Copyright 2023

All commercial rights to this Novel as a E Book, paperback, TV movie, and Cinema movies, will not be used without the written agreement of the Author and his heirs. Intellectual pirates will be pursued by all means necessary!

Richard M Sarcione

Books for Seniors

There are books for Children, Adolescents, and Adults.

Why not Books for Seniors?

Research by Gerontology Scientists at the National Institute for Aging / NIH reading stimulates the brains of Seniors, improves memory retention, and slows down the onset of Alzheimer's.

Seniors prefer paperback books over eBooks that cause electronic digital fatigue. Writers need to format their Paperback Books for Seniors with visual impairments that come with age.

Georgia 14 pt. font with increased line spacing.

150 Color 'Thumbnail Images' are intended to increase the ease and reading pleasure of my Senior Readers.

Richard M Sarcione

Heritage of Capt Isaiah Puckett and his beloved wife Hinareva

Volume One
The Puckett Adventure

A 'Whale of a Tale' your entire family will enjoy!

Whale Hunt 1885 San Francisco Chronicle

A South Pacific adventure and romance novel set in Nantucket, Tahiti, Hawaii, and the remote Marquesas islands.

Richard M Sarcione

Table of Contents

Page	Chapter
6	1 ... Nantucket Island
17	2 ... US Whaling Ship
22	3 ... Hinareva's Marriage
25	4 ... Courage and Fighting Spirit
30	5 ... Pearl Harbor Hawaii
35	6 ... Victory Flight Home
37	7 ... Tahiti-Faaa International Airport
41	8 ... The Puckett Plantation
50	9 ... The Natural Cycle of Life and Rebirth
54	10 ... An Ancient Stone Marae / Temple
65	11 ... Mama's Secret Treasure
70	12 ... Spoils of War
74	13 ... Lost Spanish Galleon
76	14 ... A New Hinano
80	15 ... Hinano's Secret Spot
86	16 ... Tahiti's National Sport
89	17 ... Love at first sight!
91	18 ... Even their va'a is invisible
93	19 ... An Old Tahitian Love Song
96	20 ... Mama Puckett's Blessing
103	21 ... Hinano's Traditional Medicine
108	22 ... Ping! Pang! Pong!

Table of Contents

Page   **Chapter**

111 ..... 23 ...Hinareva's fit of jealousy!
113 ..... 24 ...The Plantation Workshop
119 ..... 25 ... A Rising Storm
137 ..... 26 ... An Alcoholic Tyrant
141 ..... 27 ... CINCPAC Headquarters
148 ..... 28 ... Arizona Memorial
159 ..... 29 ... Te Henua Enana
168 ..... 30 ... Teiki's Marquesan Home
173 ..... 31 .... Ice Cream Frenzy!
181 ..... 32 .... A Bright New Day
195 ..... 33 .... A New Polynesian Custom
202 ..... 34 .... Teiki's Ham Radio Shack
205 ..... 35 .... Adventures of a Marquesan
207 ..... 36 .... Hollywood
214 ..... 37 .... Vietnam War
218 ..... 38 .... Fa'a'pu / Plantation Taro
223 ..... 39 .... A New Centurion Satellite
244 ..... 40 .... An Ancient Toa / Warrior Chief
248 ..... 41 .... Nantucket Island
253 ..... 42 .... My Biography

1 ... Nantucket Island

"Time to wake up!" Their Mom called out ringing the bronze ships bell hanging off the wrought iron stairs spiraling through Capt Puckett's 150 year old whaling masters home.

"Good Morning! Mom." Isaiah and Jonah said, eyeing the hot breakfast waiting on the kitchen table.

"I have your favorite breakfast." Mary Puckett said returning their good morning hugs. *"Fried flounder fillets, blueberry muffins, and hot chocolate."*

"Isaiah will make our morning prayer." Their Mom said watching her youngest son bow his head. *"Thank you, Lord, for this food we are about to eat. Amen."*

"Last night's nor'easter littered our beach with seaweed, and driftwood we need for our kitchen stove and fireplaces." Joshua Puckett called out pushing through the backdoor, pausing to warm his hands over the wrought iron stove before joining his family at the kitchen table. *"I hitched the Shetland pony to the beach buggy. We'll go beachcombing when you guys finish your breakfast."*

"Isaiah, you sit in the middle." Joshua said, lifting Isaiah on the buggy seat. *"Here's a wool blanket your Mom gave me to keep warm."*

"Your Mom packed us a picnic basket of blueberry muffins and a thermos of hot chocolate." Their Dad said, climbing aboard taking the reins, and releasing the buggy's brakes.

"Hut! Hut! Hut!" Joshua called out to his Shetland pony trotting alongside the blue-green oceanic swells curling and breaking in a thundering clap of salt spray and seafoam that stretched as far as the eye could see.

"Look at the storm debris washed up on our beach." Their Dad said, pointing at 'Salty Dog' nosing through tangles of brown kelp and driftwood.

"Search!" Jonah shouted at 'Salty Dog' digging furiously under a pile of kelp. Salty Dog is on to something!"

"It is only a piece of driftwood Dad." Jonah called back pulling the tree branch out of the seaweed.

"Break up the branch and throw the pieces in the buggy." He called out to Jonah, climbing over the backboard to rejoin his Father and Isaiah, huddling under the horse blanket to keep warm against the cold wind gusts.

8

"Search!" Jonah shouted at their Labrador Retriever digging furiously under a pile of kelp. "Salty Dog is onto something!"

"It is only a piece of driftwood, Dad." Jonah called back, pulling the tree branch out of the seaweed.

"Break it up and throw the pieces in the backboard." He called out to Jonah, climbing over the backboard to rejoin his Father and Isaiah, huddling under the horse blanket to keep warm against the cold wind gusts.

"We're in for another cold winter." Their Dad said watching Salty Dog race ahead, searching under the tangles of seaweed and driftwood tossed up on the beach. "We're still short another cord of firewood for our kitchen stove and fireplaces."

"Salty Dog discovered something!" Isaiah shouted, jumping off the buggy landing next to Salty Dog, digging up a greaseball buried in the wet sand.

"Give that to me." He growled into Salty Dog's floppy ears snatching the tasty grease ball from his jaws.

Joshua reached down with one strong hand, lifted Isaiah by the back of his collar, and plunked him down on the buggy seat.

"This is your lucky day, Son. You discovered a rare and valuable treasure! Show it to your Mom when we go home for lunch."

"What is it? Dad."

"Ambergris, Son. The regurgitated remains of giant squid eaten by sperm whales feeding in the oceanic depths off Nantucket Island."

9

"It was the ancient Egyptians who discovered how to melt down the greaseball, filter out the pure Ambergris oil, blend ylang-ylang, and other essences to make perfumes for their pharaohs."

"Today Ambergris oil is used to make the most expensive perfumes in the world."

"Beachcombing in a horse-drawn buggy has its origins in America's colonial era when fierce Atlantic hurricanes littered our beaches with the wrecks ...

... of merchant ships from Boston and New York." Joshua said handing the reins to Jonah continuing their treasure hunt along the surf breaking on their beach.

"After each hurricane, our ancestors combed our beach in their beach buggies salvaging cases of rhum, English tea, bales of cotton fabrics from our New England factories, relieving the drowned crew and passengers no longer in need of their clothing, jewelry, and money."

Pirates and Grave Robbers!

"1869 New York City newspaper article headlined how Nantucket Islanders fought each other like buzzards over the wreck of a merchant ship lost in a hurricane near our home." Joshua said, grinning at his Son's listening to him recount their more notorious ancestors' beachcombing expeditions on Nantucket Islands infamous 'Graveyard of Ships.'

"After each nor'easter, we go out in our beach buggy to search for driftwood and a new treasure." Their Dad said, whipping the reins over the Shetland pony trotting along the line of breakers crashing on the beach. *"Our Great Grandfather's 150-year-old whaling master's home is a museum of colonial-era Chippendale furniture, English and French porcelain, and American silverware from shipwrecks washed up on our ocean beaches."*

"Hut! Hut! Hut!" Joshua called out to his Shetland pony trotting along the line of waves and surf breaking on the beach.

"A pod of Sperm whales." Jonah shouted over the wind gusts. *"A half-mile off the starboard bow."*

"Let's go whale watching atop the sand dunes." Joshua called after his Sons leaping off the buggy and tethering the Shetland pony on a glass fishing buoy to graze on a patch of beach grass.

"Climb on my back, Son." Joshua said to Isaiah staring up the 100-foot high sand dune. *"I'll give you a pony ride up the sand dune."*

Jonah grabbed his Dad's fishing binoculars and struggled up the shifting sands until they scrambled over the windswept crest of the high dune.

"A family of 3 sperm whales moving slowly south." Jonah shouted, scanning the horizon with his Father's binoculars.

"Let me look too!" Isaiah shouted at his older brother.

"Tell us a whale story, Dad." Jonah asked, handing Isaiah the binoculars.

"Come sit next to me." Joshua said, placing his arms around his son's shoulders.

"Sperm whale oil is the finest lubricating oil discovered by man." Their Dad said watching Isaiah and Jonah tracking the family of cetaceans migrating south to their summer feeding grounds below the Tropic of Cancer.

"100's of barrels of fine sperm whale oil were used every day to lubricate the production machines in our New England factories manufacturing cotton textiles, leather boots, shoes, iron plows, hand tools, and arms for our new Nation." Joshua said, recounting the importance of whale oil as a **'Strategic Materiel'** transforming the United States into a modern industrial nation.

"A barrel of sperm whale oil was important to our water wheel, and steam powered industries in the 17/1800's as a barrel of fine petroleum oil from the Middle East is to today's space, automobile, and technology industries."

"By 1838 there were 13,000 whalemen aboard 273 ships from Nantucket Island, and New Bedford hunting whales in the Pacific Ocean for their 'fine' sperm whale lubricating oil, 'crude' lamp oil, ivory, ambergris, and baleen."

"Did I lose you guys in my American whaling history?" Their Dad asked pausing until he found a simple way to explain a complex idea to his sons.

"What was the 1st thing I taught you guys when your Mom and I brought you new mountain bikes for your birthday?"

"To put plenty of oil on the chain and bearings." Isaiah said, remembering his Father showing them how to oil and grease their bikes to prevent rust and saltwater corrosion.

"The 1st American bicycles were lubricated with a few drops of fine Sperm whale oil." Joshua said pleased with his whale oil lesson.

"In the 1700's Ben Franklin's printing press in Philadelphia; Eli Whitney's cotton gin in Virginia, and Daniel Boone's Kentucky rifle were lubricated with fine Sperm whale oil."

"Before every battle in the War of 1812 with King George's Royal Navy, our courageous ancestors Capt Isaiah Puckett ordered his officers, sailors, and marines to clean and swab their rifles, pistols, cannons, rifles, and cutlasses with whale oil."

"He put a few drops of whale oil on his sharpening stone to hone his cutlass to a 'razor's edge." He said, grinning at his youngest son.

"Whale oil gave our Great Grandfather a cutting edge against his English enemies on the high seas."

"Was Capt Puckett, a famous pirate like Blackbeard?" Isaiah exclaimed, slashing away at his older brother with an imaginary driftwood branch 'pirates cutlass.'

"No, Son." Joshua grinned slashing away with his driftwood cutlass to fend off his two Puckett Pirates.

"Our Great Grandfather was a famous US Navy Officer who fought with great courage against King George's Royal Navy during the War of 1812."

"Off with your pirate heads!" Joshua laughed, swinging his driftwood branch 'cutlass' in a wide arc beheading his two young Puckett Pirates.

"Araagh!" Isaiah yelled, tumbling head over heels down the dune chasing his lost head.

"Whoopee!" Jonah shouted happily, falling head over heels with his Dad in hot pursuit.

"Off your butts and on your feet!" Joshua grinned at his two Pirates playing dead at the bottom of the sand dune.

15

"Whoopee!" Jonah shouted happily, falling head over heels with his Dad in hot pursuit.

"*Off your butts and on your feet!*" Joshua grinned at his two Pirates playing dead at the bottom of the sand dune.

"*Unhitch the pony, and let's go home for lunch.*"

"*Look at the beach sand, you guys are tracking all over my clean kitchen floor!*" Mary scolded her sons and Husband.

"*We were playing pirates on the dunes.*" Isaiah exclaimed joyfully"

"What new treasure did you guys discover this morning?" Mary asked her three Puckett Pirates.

"*Salty Dog and I found this ambergris grease ball buried under a tangle of seaweed.*" Isaiah said proudly, lifting the grease ball from the wicker basket and handing it to his Mom.

"*When you go on your next shopping trip to   Boston.*" Her Husband said smiling at her.

"*Trade it at 'Panzano's deluxe 'Profumeria Boutique' for a flacon of their most expensive Italian perfume. A gift from your three Puckett Pirates.*"

"Thank you!" Mary happily. "We're having fried clams, baked potatoes, and apple pie for lunch."

"Your Mom will say her prayer before we eat." Joshua said, casting a wary eye on his two hungry Sons poised to attack their Mom's white porcelain plates filled with hot crispy fried clams.

"Thank you, Lord, for this food we are about to eat, Amen!" Their Mom said watching her Puckett pirates wait for her to finish her prayer before devouring her crispy delicacies. *"Eat heartily."*

"Wow!" She laughed, watching her family devouring her mouth-watering fried clams. *"You guys are hungry as a sperm whale devouring a school of tasty squid."*

"Your fried clams are delicious." Joshua said, trying to keep up with his Sons feeding frenzy.

*****

2 ... US Whaling Ship 'Molly Puckett'
Captain's Log : June 29, 1839

Lat. 17' 30" South, Long 149' 30" West
Tropical South Pacific Ocean. *Sunny and Warm!*

When we sailed through the narrow coral reef pass and dropped the Molly Puckett's anchor in the whaling seaport of Papeete on the Island of Tahiti. We were greeted by a flotilla of Tahitians in outrigger canoes trading fresh oranges, mangoes, and bananas to my half-starved crew.

By noon most of my whalers abandoned ship in our whaleboats and stormed ashore in search of fresh food, rum, and vahines in Papeete, a waterfront village of thatched-roof fares fringing the black sand beach fringed with coconut trees.

To provide an official presence when the Whaling Fleet drops anchor in Papeete's harbor during the three months Austral Winter. President Andrew Jackson established a US Consulate on a Paofai beachfront property given in perpetuity by the Tahitian Royal Family.

The American Consul provides seamail, legal, medical, and commercial services for the New England Whaling Masters and hundreds of whalers in port during the three month lay over.

Capt Isaiah Puckett

Captain's Log: July 1, 1839

When our whalemen start brawling in Papeete's waterfront bars and brothels, they are no match for the local mutoi / police!

To keep order ashore, our US Consul leads his Marines into the melee with clubs and rifle butts to arrest any drunk and disorderly whalers and settle any claims against them for bodily harm and property damage.

Drunk and disorderly whalemen are tried before the Consul's Court and sentenced to 3 or 4 days in his calaboose/jail. When they sober up, the Consul's Marines escort them back to their ship.

Today we began offloading our barrels of whale oil, baleen, and ivory into a local ships agency warehouse to wait for a ship sailing around Cape Horn for Boston.

This week we will haul out the 'Molly Puckett' to apply a new coat of hot coal tar on her hull."

"We need several weeks to repair our sails, rigging, and refit for our next nine-month whaling expedition in September.

Captain's Log, July 4, 1839

This morning I delivered a packet of sea mail to our US Consul and gave him a report on our last 9-month whaling expedition in the Southern Ocean.

I was invited to join a 4th of July 'Independence Day' fete on Paofai beach fronting the US Consulate.

Invited guests included New England whaling masters, local ship agents, and island traders.

A local Tahitian Arii / High Chief brought a dozen pigs, fish, taro, breadfruit, and plantains his family cooked in a ground oven dug into the black sand beach.

The laughter of the Tahitians and their children playing on the beach brought back childhood memories of our family picnics and clambakes on Nantucket beaches.

Too many years at sea, the War of 1812, whaling in the polar seas, has hardened my heart and troubled my soul.

"Wake up! Capt Puckett. You're having a bad dream!" A soft melodious voice whispered in my ear.

I could smell her Tiare Tahiti flower lei and perfumed monoi/coconut oil before I opened my eyes.

"Are you enjoying our Tahitian tamara'a / feast?" She asked curiously.

"Very much," I said, wakening slowly. *"This is the first fresh food I've eaten in months."*

"My name is Hinareva." She said watching me slowly open my eyes. *"And your name is Isaiah."*

"Everyone addresses me as Captain Puckett." I said, grinning at her lack of respect for my rank. *"Who told you my name is Isaiah?"*

"My Cousin Tamati is a harpooner on your ship." She said laughing at my chagrin.

"He says you are a tough ironfisted Whaling Master, but your officers and crew had trust and confidence in you."

"I'm not afraid of you!" She laughed. "I will call you Isaiah if I want!"

"Tell me all about your Tahitian family." I said focusing my total attention on this beautiful barefoot Vahine sitting next to me on the beach mat. "And I will tell you all about my family and home on Nantucket Island."

By late afternoon the yellow hibiscus flowers changed color and began to fall like golden snowflakes on the black sand beach. Mother Nature reminding everyone it was time to go home.

"Hinareva," I said taking her hand in mine. "I want to see you again."

"My Father says you are welcome to visit my home in Paea Village." She said, looking at her parents waiting for her in their horse-drawn carriage.

"Tomorrow, I am busy with ships business in Papeete" Isaiah said, watching her fill a pandanus bag with fresh oranges and mangoes.

"I'll come on horseback at 1st light Tuesday morning."

"We must never say goodbye, Isaiah Puckett." Hinareva smiled snatching a Tiare Tahiti flower from her hair, tucked it behind my right ear, and dashed up the beach to her parents waiting in a horse-drawn carriage.

"Each of us has a destiny to fulfill in their lifetime! Today I found mine on a small beautiful Island in the middle of the Great South Pacific Ocean!"

Isaiah Puckett

July 4th, 1839

*****

3 ... Hinareva's Marriage Fete

"You guys fell asleep last night at the beginning of your Great Grandfather's adventure in Tahiti." Their Mom said watching her Sons wolfing down her poached eggs and waffles. *"When Capt Puckett fell in love with Hinareva."*

"What happened after we fell asleep?" Jonah asked.

"At first light Capt. Puckett left Papeete on horseback and followed the bush track through the dense jungle, river crossings, and bamboo thickets to Paea Village, where Hinareva was waiting in the shade of an ancient mango tree."

"They fell madly in love and lived happily ever after!" Isaiah butted in teasing his Mother. *"Now tell us about hunting the whales! Mom."*

"Be quiet, Isaiah." Jonah demanded. *"And let Mom tell her story."*

"Capt Isaiah Puckett and Hinareva were married by the London Missionary Pastor in the Protestant church at Point Venus." Mary sighed recounting the 'Love Story' of Capt Puckett and Hinareva witnessed by the American Consul, and recorded under US law.

23

"Tahitian Arii / High Chief / Tauraatua married his beloved daughter Hinareva to her popa'a marite / white skin American by the centuries old rites in the presence of several hundred Tahitians and their families were invited to the marriage fete."

"To celebrate Hinareva's marriage her Father ordered the construction of a royal residence befitting the daughter of a Tahitian High Chief."

"The royal Tahitian fare/home was no sooner built when Hinareva gave birth to their 1st child Sarah / Manava."

"To celebrate the birth of his granddaughter Tavana / Chief Tauraatua ordered another Tamara'a/ Tahitian banquet in her honor."

"Capt Puckett's description of feasting, drinking, dancing, and debauchery has awed generations of his descendants who read his journals." Mary said, laughing at her two boys.

"What's debauchery? Mom." Jonah asked curiously.

"Ask your Father when you grow up." She chuckled. "It's what he did on R&R when he wasn't fighting the Viet Cong!"

"There's a blizzard blowing outside!" Joshua roared pushing through the kitchen door chased by a wind gust blowing snowflakes over his family.

"Two feet of snow fell last night. Six-foot snow drifts cover the roads."

"The radio says schools will be closed until further notice."

"In 1849 a smallpox epidemic ravaged Tahiti killing 1000's of Tahitians in a few months!"

"Hinareva was struck down by this terrible disease!"

"The sudden tragic loss of his beloved Hinareva broke the heart of our intrepid Capt Isaiah Puckett."

"He decided to take his oldest children, Sarah and Joshua; sail home to Nantucket having been away for ten years, buy a 2nd whaling ship for his prospering whale oil business, and return to Tahiti."

"On the return voyage, Capt Puckett contracted tuberculosis during a stopover in Brazil and died on Nantucket Island in 1852."

Sarah / Manava and Joshua / Tohora, our direct descendants, never returned to Tahiti, separating our families for over 150 years." Joshua said.

*****

4 .. Courage and Fighting Spirit

When Jonah graduated from New England University, he received a BSc in Marine Science and a Navy ROTC commission in the US Marine Corps.

1st Lt. Jonah Puckett was killed in action leading his Marine platoon against Iraqi forces during the battle of Kuwait City in 1990 and was buried with military honors in the Puckett Cemetery alongside members of his family who served with courage since the Revolutionary War.

When Isaiah walked Nantucket's cold, windswept beaches, he painfully recalled the beachcombing adventures with Jonah searching for a new treasure washed ashore after a winter storm and playing pirates atop the dunes.

A year later Mary Puckett died of cancer and was buried next to her oldest Son.

Joshua and Isaiah mourned their loss in silence, alone in their Great Grandfather's whaling master's home that weathered countless blizzards and hurricanes for over 150 years.

Isaiah grew up with his Father in their '**Puckett Boat & Bait Shop**' selling fishing tackle, live, and frozen bait to Nantucket's commercial fishermen on Nantucket Island.

In the spring, Father and Son spent their weekends and holidays upgrading their summer beach cottages for rent during Nantucket Island's three month summer tourist season.

During summer holidays, Joshua took Isaiah in their 36 ft commercial fishing boat **Mary Puckett II** into Nantucket Sound, working their lobster traps, bottom fishing for haddock and flounder, trolling for bluefin tuna, and striped bass.

Every day after school, Isaiah biked home to help his Dad in the **Puckett Boat & Bait Shop** repair their broken lobster traps, plank a holed fishing skiff, learning from his Father the marine skills passed down from each generation of Nantucket Islanders.

"What happened to you, Son?" Joshua asked looking at Isaiah's black eye.

"I had a fight after school with the high school 'Bully' Joe Higgins who likes to pick fights with anyone shorter and weaker than him."

*"*When he called me an ugly dwarf and a coward I started swinging."

"So Joe Higgins thinks we are cowardly dwarfs!" Joshua said taking his Son by the shoulders. "Let's go behind the boat shop, Son. It's time you learned to defend yourself!"

"Look at the oil painting of our Great Grandfather." Joshua said pointing at the portrait dominating the dining room.

"Capt Puckett was 5 feet, 4 inches tall. A short guy, he commanded US Navy warships and led his men in combat against the Royal Navy during the War of 1812."

"It's courage and fighting spirit that counts!" Joshua said placing a firm hand on his Son's shoulder. "Not how tall or handsome you are!"

"Rocky Marciano was a young Italian American kid from Brockton, Massachusetts." Joshua grinned at his Son. "When he was 16 years old, the local high school 'Bully' insulted his Italian heritage and beat him up."

"His Italian American Father taught him to defend himself."

"Rocky Marciano from Brockton, MA went on to become the greatest heavyweight champion boxer of all time. He won every championship fight by a knockout."

"The bigger they are!" Rocky Marciano said. "The harder they fall!"

Two hours later, Father and Son went home for a shower and dinner.

The next day after school, Isaiah failed to show at the '**Puckett Boat Shop**.' At 4 pm the telephone rang.

"Joshua, this is Paul Garrett." Chief Garrett said urgently. "Can you come right away. I have Isaiah at the Police Station."

When Joshua arrived, Chief Garrett got right to the point. *"Today, Isaiah had another fight with Joe Higgins."*

"Yesterday, Joe Higgins called Isaiah a cowardly dwarf, beat him up, and sent him home with a black eye and a bloody nose." Joshua said glaring at the Chief of Police.

"Joe Higgins is 6 feet tall and weighs over 200 lbs. He likes to pick fights with the smaller boys like my Son. Higgins is the high school 'Bully."

"Today, Joe Higgins picked another fight with Isaiah." Paul Garrett said with a grin.

"Did anyone see what happened?" Joshua asked, angrily.

"The Principal Mr. Williams and half the student body told me Isaiah hit Joe Higgins with a hard left jab to the ribs and a right uppercut to the jaw."

"Joe Higgins went down like a stone!"

"Where's the problem? Chief." Joshua demanded. *"The 'Bully' got a well-deserved beating from my Son."*

"Isaiah knocked out Joe Higgins for about five minutes." Paul said reading the Police Report.

"He was rushed by ambulance to the hospital with a broken jaw, two cracked ribs, and a concussion."

"The problem is John Higgins Father wants to charge Isaiah with assault and sue you for damages." The Chief of Police said seriously.

"I called you here to get your side of the story."

"The Principal of the High School, Mr. Williams, thinks Joe Higgins got what he deserved and has a strong case to expel the Higgins kid from High School."

"I think we can convince John Higgins to drop all charges against Isaiah in exchange for his Son returning to school on probation until the end of the school year."

"Isaiah taught the 'Bully,' a lesson he won't forget!" Paul laughed, shaking hands with Joshua and Isaiah. "Thank you, guys, for a visit."

Father and Son climbed into their pickup truck and drove to their favorite Pizza Shoppe.

"How about a pepperoni cheese pizza for dinner tonight to celebrate your 1st knockout." Joshua said, smiling at his Son.

"Rocky Marciano was right, Dad. The bigger they are, the harder they fall."

*****

5 ... Pearl Harbor, Hawaii

Isaiah graduated from New England University with a BSc. in mathematics, computer science, and a Navy ROTC Commission.

On completion of his Basic Officer Course, Ensign Puckett was assigned to a 12-month tour of shore duty as an Analyst at the 'Naval Intelligence Center,' Pearl Harbor Naval Base, Hawaii.

"It's 11 pm." He mused to himself. *"The Shore Patrol will be changing shifts or sleeping in their jeeps behind a Navy warehouse."*

Ensign Puckett gunned his 125 cc. Italian scooter in a final sprint to get to work on time.

He envied the other ensigns from his Junior Officers Course who received assignments onboard the Pacific Fleets warships in the South China Sea off the Korean Peninsula.

He and the other Ensigns finishing their one-year hardship tour at the Naval Intelligence Center dreamed about their next assignment onboard a 7th Fleet warship.

His attention was on a photo of his friend Ensign Miller in a hot tub with two naked Chinese girls in Hong Kong.

31

When suddenly, the flashing red lights of a Navy Shore Patrol jeep in his side mirror snapped him back to reality.

"Good Evening Ensign Pucket!" The Shore Patrol Petty Officer grinning as he filled in his Speeding Ticket. *"Late for work again?"*

"You were doing 45 mph in a 25 mph zone." He said laughing as he handed him the Speeding Ticket. *"This is your 3rd speeding violation in 6 months!"*

"Lucky your alcohol test is negative or we would lock you in the brig!"

"Good Night! Ensign Puckett!" The Shore Patrol called out driving off into the night.

"I must be the dumbest Ensign in the US Navy for letting the Shore Patrol trap me again!" Isaiah cursed under his breath as he parked his scooter in front of the Naval Intelligence Center.

"Good evening, Ensign Puckett." Marine Sgt Major Pete Lopez said saluting the young Navy officer. *"You're late again for work."*

"We have orders to escort you to Cmdr Hoffman. He's mad as hell and wants your head on a plate."

"Hoffman was drinking heavily before he came to work. You're not the 1st Ensign, Cmdr Hoffman menaced with a court-martial."

"Thanks for the warning, Sgt. Major."
Ensign Puckett said following his 2 Marine guards down a long damp tunnel into the warren of bunkers built after the Japanese attack on Dec. 7, 1941.

Cmdr Hoffman gave Ensign Puckett and the Marines a menacing stare when they entered his bunker, came to attention, and presented hand salutes.

"Get out!" Hoffman snarled, dismissing the Marines.

Isaiah riveted his eyes on a faded WWII photo of Admiral Bull Halsey's confident grin on the wall behind Hoffman's head gave Ensign Puckett the courage not to provoke Hoffman.

"Ensign Puckett reporting as ordered, Sir."

"Today, Ensign Puckett. You and the other Ensigns finish your one year tour of duty at the Naval Intelligence Center." Hoffman hissed in a sinister voice.

"Those I recommend will report for sea duty aboard a 7th Fleet warship when they return from their 30-day annual leave."

"I have your 1st 'Junior Officer Evaluation Report' that will be reviewed by Admiral Charles Porche, CINCPAC Chief of Naval Intelligence." Hoffman said, trying to steady the Evaluation Report in his trembling hands. *"Let me read it to you."*

33

US Navy Personnel Department
Officers Evaluation Report
Washington DC

Ensign Isaiah Puckett was assigned as an Analyst at the Naval Intelligence Center, Pearl Harbor.

Puckett holds the record for speeding violations at Pearl Harbor and is rarely on time for work.

His Intelligence reports are based on faulty data analysis and unfounded conclusions.

I recommend Ensign Isaiah Puckett II be given a 'General Discharge' from the Navy.

X ... Roy A Hoffman, Lt Cmdr
   Chief Analyst NIC
 X ....
   Charles Porche, Adm
   Director NIC

"Your 30 Day Annual Leave has been approved." Cmdr Hoffman smirked, taking a satisfactory sip from his coffee cup.

"When you return, I'll have your 'General Discharge' papers ready for your signature."

When Cmdr Hoffman failed to return his salute, Isaiah lowered his hand slowly to his side, did a quick about-face, and began the long walk up the musty tunnel past the Marine guards, into the fresh Hawaiian night air.

Isaiah paused a moment to listen to the oceanic swells breaking on the reef outside Pearl Harbor. For the 1st time in months, he could smell the sea, and it reminded him of home and family on Nantucket Island.

It was almost dawn when Isaiah pushed through the door of his BOQ, fell into a deep sleep, and dreamed of the beautiful Vahines waiting for him Tahiti and her Islands.

*****

6 ... Victory Flight Home

"Iaorana! / Welcome aboard Air Manuroa / Big Bird charter flight from Honolulu, Hawaii to Papeete, Tahiti." Vehia, the Tahitian Air Hostess, announced over the intercom.

"That must be Christmas Island." Isaiah mused, watching the jet's shadow glide across the turquoise lagoon, and plunge into the sapphire blue depths of the Great South Pacific Ocean.

"Someday, you guys must fly together to Tahiti, find and reunite our Tahitian Puckett family!" Isaiah mused recalling long-ago memories of his Father reading Capt Puckett's 'Ship's Logs' by the driftwood fire in their fireplace.

He reached into his airline bag and pulled out a color photo of Hinareva's portrait painted on canvas sailcloth brought back to his Great Grandfather's home in 1850.

Vehia watched Isaiah admiring the color photo of a beautiful young Vahine wearing an ancient necklace symbol of her rank as the daughter of a Tahitian Arii / High Chief.

Vehia looked over his shoulder. *"Is she your Vahine?"*

"She was my Great Grandmother Hinareva Tauraatua Puckett. I'm flying to Tahiti to find my Great Grandmother's family."

"Where did she live?"

"In Paea Valley 4 hours by horseback from Papeete."

A few minutes later, Vehia returned with a big smile. "Many Tauraatua and several Puckett Families are living in Paea!"

"How can I contact them?" Isaiah asked.

"Why don't you look up her family in the telephone book and call them before you try to rent a horse and buggy to take you to Paea!" Vehia laughed, double winking her eyes at him.

"Thank you very much." Isaiah said warmly. "You've been a great help!"

"We'll be landing in a few minutes." Vehia announced over the intercom. "Please fasten your seatbelts."

"The sky is blue and clear over Tahiti, temperature 27' C / 85' F, with cooling trade winds from the southeast."

"Your pilots and crew hope you enjoy your visit to Tahiti, and you will fly again with Air Manuroa."

*****

7...Tahiti-Faaa International Airport

It took Isaiah 45 minutes to go through immigration, claim his luggage, and walk into the open-air terminal.

Where 100's of cheering Tahitian supporters and their families were welcoming home their victorious canoe clubs with cheers of joy and flower leis filling the air with the fragrant scent of Tiare Tahiti / Tahiti's national flower.

After buying a $10 plastic phone card, a Tahitian mutoi / policeman directed him to a bank of telephones and a telephone book to search for his Puckett family.

Isaiah scanned down the - **P** - pages.

Puckett Pierre: 43 66 34

"Bonjour! Monsieur." Pierre responded.

"Is this the Puckett residence?" Isaiah.

"You no speak French?" Pierre demanded.

Isaiah. *"Not fluently, but I speak a little!"*

"Fiu!" Pierre retorted.

Puckett Michel: 43 57 06

When Michel answered, Isaiah, spoke first and fast!

"Is this the Puckett residence?"

"No, speak English." Michel snarled. *"Fiu!"*

Desperate, Isaiah dialed his last telephone number.

Puckett Hinano: 43 32 29

"Iaorana!" A young feminine voice answered.

"Is this the Puckett residence?" Isaiah asked taking his last chance.

"Yes, it is." Hinano said, recalling her high school English.

Isaiah. *"Do you speak English?"*

"Yes, a little." She said. *"But not very well."*

"My name is Isaiah Puckett. I've come from America to visit my family."

"I'm at Tahiti-Faaa International Airport."

"I'll be there in 30 minutes." Hinano said taking a lei and announcing.

"We have family from America coming to visit! I'm off to pick him up at the airport!"

Isaiah went into the gift shop to buy a dozen postcards of vahines sunbathing on a white sand beach: ordered a cold beer in the open-air snack bar, and began filling out his letters while he waited for his cousin Hinano.

Thirty minutes later, Isaiah spotted a rusty 20-year-old pickup truck belching clouds of diesel fumes, roar up in front of the Tahiti-Faaa Airport Terminal, and screech to a halt at the feet of an unperturbed Tahitian mutoi / policeman.

Isaiah watched a young Vahine in her 20's wearing an orange pareo, a white hibiscus flower behind her ear, a flower lei around her neck, step barefoot out of her rust-bucket pickup truck and struggle to close the door hanging precariously off the rusted hinges.

"Fiu! Fiu! Fiu!" She cursed, slamming it shut.

Hinano walked barefoot into the Airport Terminal, greeting her friends with *"Iaorana!"* A wave and a smile!

"Are you Isaiah Puckett from America?"
She asked, smiling at the short, muscular young American wearing a red Aloha shirt standing next to his luggage.

"Yes, I am." Isaiah said shaking her hand.
"And you must be Hinano Puckett."

"Iaorana! Isaiah Puckett from America."
Hinano said, placing a tiare Tahiti lei around his neck and a light welcome kiss on both cheeks.

"Welcome to Tahiti."

"We have many American programs; police, drama, and soap operas on our Tahitian television channels." Hinano laughed, double winking her eyebrows at him, and slowing her smoking rust-bucket to 35 kilometers per hour.

"On American TV, you bring your dogs, cats, and pigs into your home to live together with your family." She said wrinkling her nose. *"And you wear dirty shoes and boots in your home."*

Isaiah laughed, nodding his head in agreement.

"We keep our pigs and dogs outside, and we don't wear dirty shoes or muddy boots in our homes." Hinano said firmly. *"Please remove your shoes, leave them on the veranda before you come barefoot, into my clean house."*

"Any other important Tahitian customs I need to know?"

"I'll explain them to you when you need to know."

"Thank you, Cousin Hinano." Isaiah said. *"I will do my best to learn and respect your Tahitian customs."*

*****

8 ... The Puckett Plantation

Hinano gave a right-hand signal turning off the circle island road into a narrow bush track leading into an old coconut plantation.

"*Is that your mailbox?*" Isaiah asked spotting **'Puckett Plantation'** painted across a birdhouse mounted on a fence post.

"*That's our breadbox.*" Hinano said. "*Our local Chinese baker delivers fresh bread every morning. Mail is delivered once a week to our home by the mutoi / police/mailman on his scooter.*"

"*Our Puckett Plantation extends from the circle island road to the sea.*" She said, bouncing Isaiah on his butt as they hurtled down the bumpy bush track under the cool green canopy of the ancient coconut plantation.

"*Welcome to our Puckett home.*" She laughed, braking to a sudden stop in the shade of a breadfruit tree next to a 150-year-old plantation home.

"*Here comes our 'Welcoming Committee.*" Hinano said pointing at a pack of five uri / dogs scrambling from under the house barking and jumping on the truck's door to get a pat on the head. "*You can see they are friendly!*"

42

Suddenly! The five uri /dogs caught sight of the popa'a/ white skin stranger sitting quietly next to Hinano.

The uri leaped off the truck door and launched an assault over the bonnet, snarling and lunging at Isaiah's face through the glass windshield!

"Ta'ahoa! /That's too much!" Hinano shouted, reaching under the seat and pulled out a broom niau / made from a bundle of coconut leaf spines.

"Fa'a tea! / Get lost!" She roared shaking her broom niau in the faces of her mad dogs stopping them in their tracks.

"Before I turn you into stone door stops!"

Cold fear replaced fury in their eyes! They turned tail and disappeared under the house!

"The uri /dogs will get used to you in a few days. Until they do carry my magic broom niau to chase them away."

43

Isaiah warily opened the door and ran after Hinano with his luggage up a steep coral and lava rock stairway onto a shady veranda.

Filled with potted plants, lounge chairs, coffee tables, bamboo fishing poles, throw nets, canoe paddles, farm tools, and two jungle fowl searching for a tasty cockroach or termite hiding in the rotten wood floorboards of the century-old plantation home.

"Wake up! Mama." Hinano called to her 83 year old Grandmother sleeping in her rocking chair.

"I want you to meet Navy Ensign Isaiah Puckett II! He came from Nantucket Island in America to find his Tahitian cousins and meet their families."

Mama smiled, watching Isaiah slipping off his shoes and socks, wiggle his toes, and step barefoot on the hardwood floor.

Hinano. *"Bring your luggage and follow me." "I'll show you to our guest room."*

"Take a quick shower and a catnap until we call you for lunch."

"Where's the hot water?" Isaiah called out.

"We don't have hot water." She laughed.

Isaiah turned on the leaky water faucet and tested it before stepping under the shower. *"Brr, It's ice-cold!"*

"Lunch is ready!" Hinano called from the dining room. Isaiah slipped on a **Nantucket** t-shirt, shorts, took several gifts from his bags and stepped barefoot into the dining room where she waited with two tamari'i/ young children.

"Your Cousins! Heinui Puckett, five years old; and Temari Puckett, ten years old."

The tamari'i greeted Isaiah with a flower lei and took their seats at the mahogany dining room table filled with enough ma'a/ food to feed ten hungry Tahitians.

"I brought you several gifts from Hawaii." Isaiah said handing gift-wrapped boxes of Macadamia chocolate nuggets to Mama Puckett, Hinano, and tamari'i who immediately ripped theirs open.

Hinano glared at the tamari'i biting into Isaiah's chocolate nuggets and scolded them. *"Eat your lunch first, and save the sweets for dessert."*

"Isaiah, come sit next to me." Mama said, taking her place at the head of the table.

Hinano took her seat next to Isaiah along the dining room table decorated with a bright yellow tablecloth with a red hibiscus pattern matching the curtains on the push-out bamboo window shutters.

"We have ma'a Tahiti / Tahitian food for lunch." Mama said, pointing at three ornately carved umetes / wooden bowls.

45

"Steamed hou / green parrotfish, Uru / breadfruit, pua / pork, and fe'i / bananas smoked in our ground oven this morning."

"Taste my chopped ahi/yellowfin tuna marinated in lime juice and coconut milk." Hinano said, ladling a heaping portion of her marinated seafood delicacy on his plate.

Everyone bowed their heads while Mama made her prayer. "Thank you, Lord, for bringing Isaiah Puckett from America to visit his family in Tahiti. We ask your blessing! Amen!"

"Tama'a Maitai! / Eat Good!" She said, beaming Isaiah an angelic smile. "We eat ma'a Tahiti with our fingers. Another important Tahitian custom!"

All eyes turned to watch Isaiah eat with his fingers slick with coconut milk.

"You tell us about your Puckett family on Nantucket Island." Mama said smiling at her young Nephew from America. "And I will recount the history of our Tahitian Puckett family."

When everyone was ready, Isaiah began the history of his Puckett family that started in Tahiti more than 150 years ago. "*In 1839, my Great Grandfather Capt Isaiah Puckett sailed his* **US Whaling Ship, Molly Puckett** *into Papeete's seaport after a nine-month expedition hunting whales in the 'Roaring Forties' of the Great Southern Ocean.*"

"At a 4th of July Independence Day picnic, he fell madly in love with a beautiful Vahine Tahiti."

"Her name was Hinareva Tauraatua, daughter of Arii / High Chief Oea Raitahi Tauraatua of Paea Valley."

"They were married according to our American and your Tahitian rites and had five children; Sarah / Manava, Joshua / Matua, Thomas / Toma, Jonah / Tohora, and Rebecca / Repeta."

"In 1849 a Smallpox Epidemic swept through Tahiti and her Islands killing 1000's of pure race Tahitians including his beloved Hinareva."

"The sudden tragic loss of Hinareva broke the heart of our stalwart, Captain Puckett."

"After being gone for more than a decade, he decided to return to Nantucket Island with his two oldest children, and buy a new whaling ship for his prospering whale oil business in Tahiti."

"Capt. Puckett left his three youngest children with Hinareva's family and promised to return within two years."

"He contracted Consumption / Tuberculosis on a Brazil stopover on the return voyage and died on Nantucket Island in 1852. Here is a photo of Capt Puckett's grave in our family cemetery."

"*Put on your granny glasses!*" Hinano said smiling at her 83-year-old Grandmother. "*So, you can see the photos.*"

"*Here is a painting of Capt Puckett and Hinareva with their five children and their Tahitian Grandfather High Chief / Ari'i Nui Oea Raitahi Tauraatua.*" Isaiah said, handing the color prints to Mama. "*My favorite is Hinareva's portrait by Robert Pratt captures her radiant natural beauty that has enchanted generations of our family.*"

"*She is wearing the pearl shell and whale ivory emblem that defines her status as the daughter of the royal family that rules Paea valley and her magical power to heal or destroy her enemie.*"

"*Do you have any photos of your family and home on Nantucket Island?*" Hinano asked Isaiah opening the 3rd envelope.

"*These photos were taken at our annual Nantucket family reunion and clambake held every summer on the beach fronting our home.*" He said recalling a flood of childhood memories growing up on Nantucket Isaiah said recalling the sorrow and loss of his Mother and Brother.
"*My older brother, 1st Lt. Jonah Puckett USMC, was killed in the Gulf War.*"

"You miss your family." Hinano whispered, looking at the sorrow in Isaiah's eyes.

"This is my Great Grandfather's tombstone." He said, handing Mama the photo.

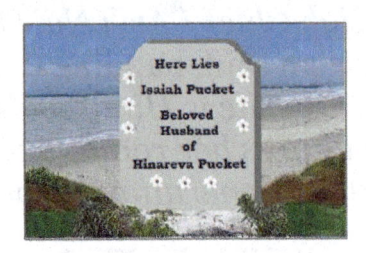

> Here Lies
> Isaiah Puckett
>
> Beloved
> Husband
> of
> Hinareva Puckett

When Mama read Capt Puckett's epitaph, she recalled long-forgotten childhood memories when she and her parents cleaned the weeds and grass off their family cemetery. Placed a fresh bouquet on each grave and said a prayer to honor the memory of each loved one.

Her voice trembled, and tears rolled down her face when she read Captain Puckett's last words engraved on the tombstone.

"Beloved Husband of Hinareva Puckett"

"The emotional shock is too much for her!" Hinano called out to her family to give a helping hand. *"Help me carry her into the bedroom!"*

Ten minutes later, Hinano returned to her family, waiting anxiously on the veranda. *"Mama is resting quietly."*

49

"She needs a good night's sleep, and tomorrow morning she'll be fine."

"Good morning, Mama." Isaiah asked. "How do you feel this morning?"

"Much better." She smiled holding the photo of Hinareva close to her heart. *"Your photos brought back long forgotten emotional memories."*

"I have your favorite fish for breakfast." Hinano said, placing two pan-fried ature / mackerel on her plate.

"I hope you like our Tahitian breakfast!" She said placing a hot ature on his plate. *"Taste our Tahitian coffee with fresh coconut milk. You have a choice of hot coconut bread or firi firi / our Tahitian doughnuts."*

"I hope someday you and Mama will visit our home on Nantucket Island. My Dad and I will cook our favorite fish for breakfast."

"Flounder fillets fried in garlic butter served with my Mom's secret tartar sauce."

*****

9 ... The Natural Cycle of Life and Rebirth

"For generations, our Puckett Plantation was the most productive in Tahiti." Mama said, leading Hinano and Isaiah into a narrow footpath under the overgrown plantation that was once the domain of fat dairy and beef cattle grazing on well-tendered pastures, orange groves, and taro paddies.

"My Husband Manu, our 3 Sons, and I worked from dawn to dusk in our plantation as did generations of my family before us."

"When my Tane died in 1975, my Sons lost interest in our plantation and were lured away by high salaries and soft government jobs in Papeete."

"Trying to keep our Puckett Plantation productive was too much work for a Vahine ruau / elderly Vahine and her Granddaughter." She said, looking up at the aging coconut trees overgrown with Spanish moss. *"Mother Nature is reclaiming her domain in the natural cycle of death and rebirth.*

Isaiah followed Mama and Hinano until they walked into the bright morning sunlight shining on a flower garden next to a natural spring bubbling into an oval lava rock basin.

51

Hinano scooped a coconut shell of cold spring water and offered it to Mama and Isaiah.

"This is our flower plantation!" Hinano said, leading Isaiah on a short walking tour of carefully tendered rows of red torch ginger, golden bird of paradise, and orchids Mama brought to sell in **Papeete's Public Market** every few days in Hinano's pickup truck.

"Help me with this bouquet." She said, handing Isaiah a plastic bucket filled with red torch ginger, and golden bird of paradise flowers.

"Follow me!" Mama smiled, pulling a worn bush knife from a rotten tree stump and continuing along the footpath until they came to another clearing.

*"This is our **Puckett Family Cemetery**."* She said leading Isaiah past rows of white headstones.

"This is my Husband, Manu's grave." Mama stood, facing her Husband's tombstone and began a short prayer. *"When I die, I want you to bury me next to him."*

"I promise!" Hinano whispered, embracing her.

Hinano and Isaiah stood back watching Mama probe with her bush knife under brown roots and decaying leaves until she found a dozen black lava stones indicating the grave of a long-forgotten ancestor.

The Puckett Vahines stood in silence watching Isaiah chop away the strong guava roots clearing the dark topsoil off an ancient headstone laying face down in the dark earth.

"Stand it up." Mama ordered.

Hinano pleaded. *"Don't let this popa'a / white skin foreigner desecrate our ancestor's tomb!"*

Horrified, Hinano stood behind Mama watching Isaiah dig the ancient headstone free and struggle to lift it upright.

"It's too heavy." Isaiah grunted, looking up at Mama.

"Hinano, help Isaiah stand up that headstone."

Hinano swallowed her fear and obeyed her Grandmother. She knelt in the brown soil, and together they slowly pushed the headstone upright.

Tears welled in Isaiah's eyes as he read his Great Grandfather's 1849 epitaph, his loving hands chiseled in stone.

Here lies Hinareva Puckett.
Beloved wife of Isaiah Puckett

"I will remember this moment as long as I live. Thank you for showing me Hinareva's final resting place."

"I made this bouquet of fresh flowers to put on her grave." Mama said, handing him a bouquet of red torch ginger, anthuriums, and orchids Isaiah arranged in clay flower pots next to Hinareva's headstone.

"Let's bow our heads in silent prayer in memory of our beloved ancestor Hinareva who rests in peace with us today." Mama whispered, watching Isaiah's tears of joy fall like raindrops and embrace Hinareva's heart and soul.

*****

10 ... An ancient stone Marae / Temple

"Follow me. I have more to show you." She said, continuing their walk into a thicket of ferns hiding a raised courtyard of lava rocks with a 10-foot wall of coral and basalt blocks dominating an ancient temple site.

"This ancient ruin is our Tauraatua marae/ temple." She said pointing into the overgrown temple. *"On this sacred marae, our ancestors prayed to our ancient gods to protect us from cyclones and guide our voyaging canoes when we set sail to visit our families in Hawaii and Aotearoa / New Zealand."*

"Can I go take a close look at our marae/temple?"

"Yes." Mama smiled. *"But don't touch or disturb anything. This marae is a sacred temple that contains the bones of our ancestors and the spirits of our gods."*

"Are you coming with me, Cousin Hinano?"

"No, the marae is off-limits to vahines!"

Isaiah chopped his way through the dense tangle of vines and banyan tree roots until he reached the 10-foot high double wall of massive coral and basalt blocks Mama said was the ahu / sacred sepulcher for the spirits and bones of our gods and ancestors.

55

"One hundred fifty years ago." Capt Puckett scribed in his Tahiti Journals.
"This marae/temple was the center of a 1000 year old Polynesian civilization for a proud race who lived in peace and harmony with nature until the first Europeans arrived to impose their language, bible, culture; and colonial rule by the musket, bayonet, cannon, and disease.

"Any Tahitian who violated the mana / spiritual force of the Tahua / High Priest would die in three days!" Capt Puckett observed first hand.

"Today." His Great Grandson observed.
"This marae is a lost archaeological ruins of an ancient civilization whose sole remaining inhabitants are an army of menacing Tupa / land crabs who stand guard over every rock and crevice with open claws ready to defend their sacred temple against any intruder.

"The sun is high." Hinano called out across the marae. "Time to go back!"

Isaiah retraced his path through the ruins to Hinano and Mama Puckett sitting in the shade of a gnarled century-old orange tree devouring a half dozen fresh-picked oranges.

"You were right, Mama." Isaiah said wiping the sweat off his brow. *"The banyan tree roots pushed aside the coral and basalt rocks, and I could see hundreds of skulls and bones inside ahu /altar."*

"Did you see any tu pau-pau/ghosts inside the ahu?" Hinano asked fearfully.

"No, but when the Tupa crabs scurried out of the golden skulls across the loose bones, they made a loud, **Clack! Clack! Clack!** *death rattle that gave me a real fright!"* He laughed watching Hinano's eyes wide open.

"It was hot, humid, and teeming with nao-nao / mosquitos!"

"Taste one of our oranges!" Hinano smiled, offering him a dozen juicy slices on a banana leaf.

"Exploring the overgrown marae gave me a real thirst." Isaiah said devouring a half dozen orange slices. *"Your oranges are sweet and juicy!"*

"Thank you, Cousin Hinano!"

"Look carefully, Isaiah." Mama said, pointing into the century-old orange grove.

"More than 100 orange trees are producing delicious sweet oranges that fall and rot on the ground."

"The young Tahitian men who follow Hinano home take one look at the work to clear this old plantation." She said looking at her Granddaughter. *"They run back to their soft government jobs in Papeete!"*

Isaiah, *"I will find my Cousin Hinano a rugged cowboy from Texas to turn your Puckett Plantation into a modern, profitable agribusiness."*

Furious! Hinano turned heel and dashed off in a huff down the footpath. *"Tonight, Isaiah Puckett!"*

"You can sleep under the house with the uri and the nao-nao!"

"I'll never understand women." Isaiah mused, scratching his head at Hinano's fit of temper.

"When Hinano gets mad at you!" Mama laughed after Hinano rushing off into the jungle footpath. *"She will chase after you with her broom niau."*

"When you see a Vahine Tahiti grab her broom niau." She said, laughing after Isaiah.

"You Tanes / men better run for your life!"

"That's another important Tahitian custom you better not forget."

"I won't forget." Isaiah said, remembering how Hinano struck fear in the eyes of her mad dogs with her magic broom niau.

"It's high noon, young man. Let's go home for lunch."

"Hinano will have punu pua'a toro / corned beef, and uru / breadfruit for lunch, and I'm ready for my afternoon nap."

Isaiah, "You look tired, Mama, we'll take our time walking back to the house."

When they reached the bottom of the stairs, he spotted Hinano waiting on the veranda, pointing her magic broom ni'au straight at him.

Mama paused a moment at the bottom of the stairs to recount another facet of her families history.

"To celebrate Hinareva's marriage with Capt Puckett, our High Chief /Ari'i Nui ordered the construction of a royal residence befitting the beloved princess of an Ari'i nui / Tahitian King."

Mama Puckett paused a moment at the bottom of the stairs to recount another facet of her families history.

"To celebrate Hinareva's marriage with Capt Puckett, our High Chief /Ari'i Nui ordered the construction of a royal residence befitting the beloved princess of an Ari'i nui / Tahitian King."

"The Royal Fare was built on a raised platform of lava rocks and ornately carved aito / ironwood posts, and uru / breadfruit beams held up an immense thatched roof woven from the best pandanus leaves from the Island of Mai'ao."

"A few years later, after a tropical cyclone devastated Tahiti."

"Capt Puckett and his whalers built a new plantation home on solid ironwood posts 8 feet above the original lava rock platform you can see underneath our home."

"A tin roof replaced the pandanus roof, electricity, and plumbing as the times required, but we haven't changed his original plan."

"This is your Great Grandfather and Princess Hinareva's original Royal Tahitian Palace!" Mama said, taking Isaiah's arm and walking up the stairs on the veranda where Hinano waited to greet them with her broom ni'au/ magic wand.

"You look and smell like a Billy Goat, Isaiah Puckett."

"You need a cold shower to wash off your sweat and smell bad!" Hinano said, pointing her broom niau at the Billy Goat from Nantucket Island.

"We'll eat lunch when you are sparkling, clean, and smell good. Another important Tahitian custom."

"Haere mai tamaa! / Come eat with us!" Mama called out from the dining room.

Isaiah slipped on a clean **Hawaii** t-shirt, shorts, followed the delicious aroma coming from the dining room, and sat down next to Hinano.

"Maruru ete fatu no te ie maa ota ma otou e faa nei nei ite amu. / Thank you, Lord for this food we are about to eat. Amen." Mama whispered giving Isaiah and Hinano her famous angelic smile.

"Tamaa maita'i! / Eat well!"

Hinano opened two large Uru wrapped in banana leaves and cut them in half with a razor-sharp piece of bamboo. "Be careful. They're steaming hot."

61

"The New England whalers introduced corned beef and onions to Tahiti." Mama said, scooping Isaiah, a plate of pan-fried corned beef and onions. *"We Tahitians added the breadfruit."*

After lunch, Isaiah helped Hinano clear the table and wash the dishes while Mama went into her bedroom for her siesta.

"Let's go sit on the veranda and have a snack while we wait for Mama to wake up from her nap." Hinano said, handing Isaiah a pitcher of iced tea and a plate of ice-cold pineapple slices to carry on the veranda.

"What did you put in the iced tea?" Isaiah asked, savoring a long cold drink.

"Shave ice, a pinch of vanilla, and a slice of green lime." She smiled, refilling his glass and offering him a plate of pineapple slices. *"Taste our Tahitian pineapple we grow on our plantation."*

"Your Tahitian pineapple is delightful!" Isaiah said helping himself to a half dozen slices. *"Our Hawaiian pineapple is a genetically modified variety to be canned or made into juice."*

"We grow a sweet variety of pineapple to eat fresh." Hinano said, watching Isaiah finish the last slice.

Isaiah, *"Do you like being a primary school teacher?"*

"Oh, yes! It's fun working with 5 to 8-year-old children."

"My Paea Primary School is a ten minute walk from home so I can keep a close eye on my Grandmother."

"I have a good salary and a five week vacation every year."

"Do you like being an Ensign in the US Navy?"

"I'll bet you travel all over the Pacific in a warship and have a Vahine in every port of call."

"I joined the Navy to see the world like my Great Grandfather, not buried in an underground bunker." Isaiah said painfully.

"My boss Cmdr Hoffman is an alcoholic tyrant who takes a sadistic pleasure in terrorizing his Ensigns. I've had a difficult tour at Pearl Harbor."

"I'm Fiu! /I've had enough. I'm ready to resign from the Navy and do something else with my life."

"I'm sorry you had a bad experience." Hinano said, seeing the pain in his eyes.

"Did you have a good nap?" Isaiah asked, following Hinano into Mama's bedroom.

"Yes, a short nap after lunch recharges my 83-year-old battery." She laughed. "I feel much better now!"

63

"Coming to Tahiti to search for my Tahitian family has been a wonderful experience!"

"I'm delighted I found you, Mama Puckett, and the heritage Capt Puckett and Hinareva left for our descendants."

"It's been a real adventure and pleasure to unite our families after more than 160 years."

"Hinano!" Mama called out from her bedroom.

"I need a helping hand. Would you and Isaiah come in here for a minute."

"Did you have a good nap?" Isaiah asked, following Hinano into Mama's bedroom.

"Yes, a short nap after lunch recharges my 83-year-old battery." She laughed. "I feel much better now!"

"Would you pull out my old steamship trunk?" She asked, pointing to an old steamer trunk hidden away in her closet.

"Did this old trunk belong to Capt Puckett?"

"No! Isaiah." She laughed. "His sea chest was destroyed by termites and fungus when I was a little girl."

"I bought this one in 1940 when Manu and I took a three-month honeymoon cruise on a Matson Line steamship to San Francisco."

"We stayed in San Francisco's finest hotels, went on a shopping spree, rode the famous cable cars to the stars, feasted on steamed crab at Fisherman's Wharf, and dined in the best Chinese and Italian restaurants."

"We bought and shipped home a new Ford pickup truck and a farm tractor to use on our plantation."

Hinano, "You never told me you went to San Francisco!"

Mama laughed at Hinano, interrupting her story!

"It was an adventure driving our new pickup truck to sell our coffee, vanilla, oranges, flowers, and farm produce in Papeete's Public Market and then go on shopping in the Chinese Quarter."

"Would you open my steamship trunk." She said, handing Isaiah the brass key. "I have something to show you."

*****

65

11 ... Mama's Secret Treasure

"When was the last time you opened this steamship trunk?" Isaiah laughed, forcing the key to unlock the rusty padlock while Hinano struggled to raise the trunk lid on its squeaky hinges.

Mama pushed Isaiah aside and began rummaging inside her steamer trunk until she found a silk dress she lovingly handed to Hinano. *"This is my wedding dress, try it on later, and see if it fits you."*

"Someday, Cousin Hinano." Isaiah smiled trying to please. *"You'll make some lucky man a beautiful bride in Mama's white silk wedding dress."*

Hinano was not amused!!

"I'll never understand women." Isaiah shrugged, watching Hinano glare at him.

"Lift out my sandalwood chest." Mama ordered Hinano. *"Carry it into the dining room and place it on the table."*

"Isaiah! Lift out the walnut case and place it on the table."

"Did you bring your Puckett Family Genealogy?" Mama asked, placing a roll of goatskin parchment on the table.

"When my husband died and my Sons left, I was alone in this plantation house with only the tupa'u'pa'u/ ghosts of our ancestors to keep me company."

"To spice up my life, I went on holiday to Bora Bora. I stayed with the Tamatoa family with 11 children. Their newborn was a baby girl only five weeks old."

"Her name was Hinano! It was love at first sight! She was the daughter I always dreamed of raising!"

"After several weeks, her mother proposed I fa'a'amu/ adopt baby Hinano and take her home with me to Tahiti, where I raised Hinano as my fa'a' mu / adopted granddaughter." Mama sighed taking Hinano's hand in hers. *"Her biological parents live on the island of Bora Bora."*

"Hinano Tamatoa Puckett has no biological relationship with our Puckett family. Do you understand this?"

Isaiah scratched his head until clarity replaced confusion. *"Fa'a'amu / adoption! Another important Tahitian custom. Now I understand why she gets furious when I call her 'Cousin' Hinano!"*

Hinano's eyes blazed with a radiance that made Isaiah's heart jump! *"Tomorrow, you're going to discover a new Hinano."*

"This walnut case belonged to your Great Grandfather." Mama said, pointing to the walnut case he recognized from a similar one he had seen in the US Navy Museum at Annapolis, Maryland.

Isaiah read the inscription on the bronze plate:

US Navy Sextant Serial No 1786
Capt Isaiah Puckett
1812

"Maururu! / Thank you! Mama !" Isaiah said, taking her in a warm embrace.

Isaiah opened the cover, lifted out the bronze sextant, and placed it to his eye as he had trained using the Navy's standard plastic sextant.

"I will cherish my Great Grandfather's sextant and use it to navigate across the oceans with the same accuracy and precision as he did in his lifetime at sea."

Hinano looked at Mama, wondering what new surprise awaited inside the red sandalwood treasure chest.

"Hinano, could I have another glass of pineapple juice before we open my next surprise."

Hinano looked at Mama, wondering what new surprise awaited inside the sandalwood chest.

"Hinano, could I have another glass of pineapple juice before we open my next surprise. Mix in a shot of rhum to thin out my tired blood and relieve the aches and pains that come with old age."

The 83-year-old Arii Vahine Ru'au/ Queen Mother took her time savoring her ice-cold rum punch until she was ready to reveal her next surprise! *"For medicinal purposes only!"*

Hinano began pushing the sandalwood chest across the table to Isaiah when her Grandmother stopped her.

"No! Hinano, it's not for him. Open the chest, take out the yellow envelope in your name, and read us the document."

Tears welled up in Hinano's eyes when she began reading her Grandmother's handwritten notarized document.

Last Will and Testament

Ahu'ura Tetuanui Puckett

I Ahu'ura Tetuanui Puckett, being of sound mind and body on my 83rd Birthday, do solemnly bequeath to my fa'a'mu / adopted Granddaughter, Hinano Puckett.

My personal property, home, and title to my Puckett Plantation on the attached Land Title and Surveyors Plan at the Government Land Office in Papeete, Tahiti.

Witnessed by my 2 Sons: Hiro and Temauri Pucket

By my hand and signature:
Ahu'ura Tetuanui Puckett

69

When Hinano finished reading Mama Puckett's Last Will, she reached out, taking her Grandmother in a warm embrace.

"Are you happy?" Isaiah asked softly.

"We're delighted!" Mama and Hinano whispered.

Hinano wiped away her tears of joy, and carefully placed her Grandmother's legacy in the sandalwood chest.

"We're not finished!" Mama said shaking her head. *"Pull out the top tray."*

*****

12 ... Spoils of War

"Capt Puckett gave this sandalwood chest to Hinareva. His legacy to each new generation of his female descendants." Mama said, recounting Capt Puckett's codicil to Hinareva. *"Now it's my turn to pass this sandalwood chest to my granddaughter Hinano. Pull out the bottom tray and look inside."*

Hinano pulled out three sailcloth bags and emptied them one by one on the dining room table.

"Wow!" Isaiah called out, staring at three piles of gold jewelry encrusted with pearls, rubies, saphires, and diamonds sparkling in the sunlight shining through the windows.

"Capt Puckett bequeathed this treasure to his beloved wife, and Hinareva's female descendants." Mama said remembering her Mother's instructions. *"His legacy to their daughters, and passed down to each generation of Puckett Vahines."*

"Capt Puckett's codicil was clear: Use this treasure wisely to care for your children and build your family fortunes."

"Do you know the history of this fabulous treasure?" Mama asked her Nephew. "It's been an enigma and a mystery to every generation."

"We've kept this a family secret because we were afraid of it."

"This treasure scares me!" Hinano called out.

"How did Capt Puckett acquire this treasure hunting whales in the Southern Ocean? Was he a Pirate Captain before he came to Tahiti?"

Isaiah started laughing! "When the War of 1812 broke out between the United States and England, our Great Grandfather fought against the Royal Navy on the high seas in fierce naval battles off the American Coast and the British Isles."

"The War of 1812 was mainly a naval war between the US Navy and King George's Royal Navy using cannon and grapeshot at close range to sink each other's warships before they fought to the death with rifles, pistols, bayonet, and cutlass."

"This type of combat was brutal, with no quarter given by the Americans or their English enemies. King George never accepted the United States as an independent nation but rather a renegade colony to be punished at all costs."

"When his good friend, Capt John Smedley, was tried as an American pirate before an English Admiralty Court in Portsmouth and hanged on a yardarm."

"CaptPuckett swore vengeance on every English officer in the Royal Navy expecting them to defend to the death with pistol and cutlass the superior colonial interests of King George and England."

"With a stroke of his cutlass, he cut off their jewelry, rings, and medals that showed their rank as aristocratic royalty." Isaiah said, grinning at a horrified look on Mama and Hinano's faces.

"He seized their wealth, gold ingots, and jewelry on the captured English ships as his personal 'Spoils of War."

"I hope this explains Capt Puckett's treasure." He said, smiling at Hinano and Mama.

"Capt Puckett's fearless leadership in the War of 1812, courage in the battle against his enemies, and heroic adventures leading whaling expeditions to the far corners of this planet have inspired every generation who followed him."

"I'm sure Hinareva is pleased I pass down this emblem of her magic power as a Tahu'a/ Sorceress." Mama said, beginning an ancient Tahitian chant that for a moment absorbed Hinano's spirit as she slowly lifted an antique necklace woven from human hair and whale ivory, from the sandalwood chest and fastened it around Hinano's neck.

"What have you done to her?" Isaiah staring at Hinano, smiling at him as if nothing had happened.

"I've passed my magic power as Tahu'a / Sorceress down to my Granddaughter."

"What's a Tahua?" Isaiah asked, staring at Mama.

"It means." Hinano laughed. *"I can fly after you on my broom niau on Halloween!"*

"You still have many things to learn about your Tahitian family as we have to learn about your American family with your strange pirate customs." Mama said, double winking her eyebrows at her perplexed Nephew.

*****

13 ... Lost Spanish Galleon

"In his ***Personal Journals***,' Capt Puckett described sailing the '***Molly Puckett*** 'in search of a Spanish galleon wrecked in a fierce Tropical Cyclone on a reef in the Tuamotu Atolls." Isaiah said examining the mint seal stamped into the 24-carat gold ingots.

"He found the wreck, but it was beyond the depth his Tahitian pearl divers could go without getting the bends. He gave it up when one of his Tahitian divers became paralyzed and nearly died from diving too deep."

"He recorded his search for the wreck of the lost Spanish galleon in an **1839 Personal Journal** in a **1812 US Navy Code** lost in time."

"Is this his secret journal?" Mama asked, taking a 'Personal Journal' out of the sandalwood case and handing it to Isaiah.

Isaiah thumbed through the coded pages, then looked at Mama. "I can't be sure until I find the 1812 Navy code to decipher it."

"What is this soft white rock encrusting the gold coins and ingots?"

"It's coral that grew on them when they were in the sea." Hinano grinned, sniffing her coral encrusted treasure.

"He found the wreck, but it was 200 feet deep at the limit for the pearl divers to free dive without risking death."

"He didn't want to risk the Tahitian pearl divers lives for the Conquistadors gold, so he sailed home with Hinareva and his children to Tahiti." Hinano said looking at Isaiah with a visionary glow in her eye. "Capt Puckett was already a wealthy man."

"He encrypted his secret in this journal and left it as a challenge and quest for his male descendants."

"Everything I own is now passed down to my beloved Granddaughter." Mama said pressing the key in Hinano's hand and taking her in a warm embrace. "We've closed the circle to the past."

"Place everything into my treasure chest and carry it into my bedroom."

*****

14 ... A New Hinano

It was almost dawn when Isaiah awakened to the distant rumble of oceanic swells breaking on the coral reef, and the aroma of Tahitian coffee and frying fish.

"Good Morning!" Isaiah said smiling at Hinano singing and flipping fish to the rhythm of Esther Tefana's latest CD. *"You're happy this morning."*

"I like to sing along with Esther when she sings love songs from the Tuamotu Atolls. **Esther Tefana is the 'Voice of Tahiti and her Islands!"**

Isaiah, *"Before I fly back to Hawaii, I'll buy several of her CD's to remind me of my visit to Tahiti."*

"Where's Mama this morning?"

"She left before dawn with a pickup truck of fresh flowers to sell in Papeete's open-air Public Market." Hinano said, pouring Isaiah a cup of Tahitian coffee.

"We're having fried lagoon fish and breadfruit chips for breakfast." She smiled, smacking her lips.

"Your Tahitian coffee and fish smell delicious!" Isaiah said, taking his first sip.

"Do you make a prayer before meals?" She asked.

"Not since my mother died."

"You're a heathen, Isaiah Puckett!"

"I promise to respect your Tahitian custom and wait for you to make a prayer before I touch the food." He said, waiting for Hinano to bow her head and begin her morning prayer.

*"What would you like to do today? I'm an excellent tour guide. We could take my pickup to our historic '**Point Venus Beach Park**,' or we could visit our '**Museum of Tahiti and her Islands**!"*

"Let's go sightseeing another day." Isaiah chuckled at the thought of another death-defying ride in Hinano's rust-bucket pickup truck.

"I just want to spend a quiet day with you relaxing on the beach."

"I'll be ready in a few minutes!" She said, dashing off to her bedroom.

Isaiah changed into a **US NAVY** t-shirt, white shorts, reef shoes, pulled on a floppy sun hat; packed his mask, fins, snorkel into his dive bag; and walked on the veranda to wait for Hinano.

"How do you like the new Hinano?" Hinano asked, prancing barefoot on the veranda and pirouetting around her young American Ensign.

"You look magnificent!" Isaiah said admiring her natural Polynesian beauty that made our Vahine Tahiti world-famous in prose, paintings, music, and cinema.

"A radiant Polynesian smile." Isaiah said happily beginning his Vahine Inspection. *"A gardenia flowerhead crown. A great natural perfume."*

"Black silky hair that falls almost to her butt."

"A bright orange and white pareo/sarong, I can almost see-through."

"A nicely rounded butt that dances when she prances."

"Bare feet, exceptionally clean."

"A classic Vahine Tahiti!" Isaiah said, concluding his Vahine Inspection.

"I've never seen you wearing makeup." He said, smiling at Hinano enjoying his close up inspection.

"I rarely wear makeup."

"Two ripe tropical fruit!" He said, admiring her firm oval breasts straining against her pareo.

She laughed, pushing him away.

"When I was a Tamahine / Little Girl, we could see the coral reef, lagoon, and Moorea from our veranda." Hinano said, picking up her bamboo fishing pole, bush knife, beach mat, and paddles.

"Follow me!" She said, leading him into a narrow footpath through the purau thicket to the beach 200 feet from the plantation home. *"Now, our backyard is overgrown with hibiscus trees."*

"The view from your beach is awesome!"
Isaiah called out enjoying the sweeping panorama of white sand beach fringed with tall coconut trees swaying in the cool trade winds blowing across an immense turquoise lagoon teeming with tropical fish and corals.

Blue oceanic swells curling and thundering across the reef, and the distant white clouds above the emerald green island of Moorea shimmering on the distant horizon.

*****

15 ... Hinano's Secret Spot

Isaiah followed Hinano along the beach into the shade of a hibiscus tree covered with 100's of bright yellow flowers.

"This is 'Hinano's Secret Spot!" She said spreading her pandanus beach mat on the white sand next to her outrigger canoe.

"This is the 1st chance I've had to recuperate and rest since I joined the Navy." Isaiah yawned stretching out on Hinano's beach mat, looked up at two snow white fairy terns alighting on a tree top branch, closed his eyes, and fell into a deep sleep.

Hinano sat down next to her Prince Charming sleeping soundly on her beach mat.

"I wonder if he's dreaming of me?" She mused waving her gardenia flower under his nose.

"Yes! He is!" She giggled watching him smile up at her.

"Now it's my turn to inspect you!" Hinano giggled beginning her Tane Inspection by tracing her fingers lightly across his chest.

"He's a short, muscular Tane with a gentleness inherited from Hinareva."

"The resemblance to Capt Puckett is amazing. He has his Great Grandfather's pirate head, black hair covers his chest and arms."

"The same hawk nose. The same bullheaded determination and courage."

"He's dead to this world." She giggled, tracing her finger lightly around the bulge in his shorts.

"Oh my, he's hung like a Billy Goat!" She whispered. *"Sweet dreams, my young Pirate Prince!"*

"I'll go fishing behind the reef while he sleeps." She mused placing her bamboo fishing pole, fishing bag, hoe/paddle in her va'a/ outrigger canoe, and started pushing her va'a on two coconut log rollers down the white sand beach into the lagoon.

She glanced over her shoulder at Isaiah, sleeping under the purau / hibiscus tree and began paddling across the lagoon.

"It's a perfect morning to catch lagoon fish." She mused, dropping her stone anchor in the wave surge cascading off the reef crown, baited her hook with a shrimp, watching it sink slowly under a coral head, and waited for her first bite.

Hinano opened a cough syrup bottle filled with monoi scented with sun-dried ylang-ylang, taporo / lime, and tiare Tahiti flowers; slipped off her pareo, smoothing it on her face, arms, and legs to keep her skin soft, moist, and prevent sunburn.

"I hope he likes my monoi!" She giggled massaging the perfumed coconut oil into her mango shaped breasts.

"Ummm! It smells good and makes me feel sexy."

A sudden tug on her bamboo fishing pole snapped her out of her daydream!

She pulled hard on her bamboo pole and a blue green uhu / parrot fish came flopping into the outrigger canoe!

   Several parrot fish later she glanced back at Isaiah sitting under the purau tree photographing her with his camera and telephoto lens.

Wearing only a smile, a white gardenia behind her ear, teeny weeny string bikini, Isaiah watched her paddle through the labyrinth of coral heads, and step out at the water's edge.

"Hold up your string of fish so I can take a photo to send to my Dad!" Isaiah called out snapping a half dozen digital photos with his camera.

"Start collecting dry branches, and light a fire on the bed of lava stones under the purau tree." Hinano said cleaning her fish at the water's edge.

83

"*Happiness is a lunch of tasty barbecued blue green parrotfish.*" She laughed happily.

"*Did you enjoy my barbecued parrotfish?*" She asked, tearing apart the fish head with her teeth and sucking out the tasty meat.

"*Let me help you.*" Hinano said, popping tasty morsels in his mouth.

"*It was delicious, but now I'm very thirsty.*"

Hinano picked up her bush knife and pulled him to his feet. "*Come with me 'Tarzan' Tane we'll go cut down 4 or 5 pape ha'ari!*"

"*What's a pape ha'ari?*"

"*A green drinking coconut.*" She laughed, leading him to a coconut tree pushed over by a recent cyclone growing horizontal to the beach, climbed on the trunk, and tight walked over to a bunch of young green coconuts hanging off the treetop.

"*You look like 'Tarzana' in your string bikini!*" Isaiah called up admiring Hinano cutting off a dozen green coconuts with swift strokes of her bush knife.

"*The next time 'Tarzan Tane,' you climb half-naked up the tree and cut down the pape ha'ari while I stand below and admire your two hairy coconuts!*"

She laughed, tossing down a green coconut, making him jump aside to avoid her guided missile.

"*Hold it up like this,*" She said pushing his hands and the coconut up in the air.

"*You're spilling it all over yourself!*" She giggled, watching the sweet coconut water spill off his chin, stream down his hairy muscular chest and stomach muscles, cascade over his shorts, and disappear in the beach sand.

"*It's real, sweet, and refreshing.*" He gurgled finishing his first pape ha'ari.

Hinano, "*You're covered with black curly hair on your neck, shoulders, arms, and legs.*"

"*You even have tufts of black hair growing out of your ears like a Billy Goat.*"

"It's the pirate blood in my family."

"*Capt Puckett's father was a Portuguese African pirate shipwrecked on Nantucket Island in the 1700s after a fierce Atlantic hurricane.*"

Two snow-white fairy terns, watched Isaiah place his arms around Hinano's neck, and meet her lips in a first lovers kiss.

"You're the most extraordinary young woman I have ever met." Isaiah said from the bottom of his heart. *"I'll always remember this first kiss with you."*

Hinano held her lover in a long embrace.

"Stop." She laughed, pushing his face and hands away from her ripe mangoes.

"Another important Tahitian custom. No sex on the beach! There are always children playing nearby."

"Let's walk back to my va'a and eat a few mangoes for dessert." Hinano said, taking him by the hand to her 'Secret Spot' next to the outrigger canoe.

"We have several mango trees in our backyard." She said, peeling and offering two golden ripe fruit to Isaiah. *"They're juicy and sweet."*

*****

16 ... Tahiti's National Sport

"Your va'a looks like it came from a museum." Isaiah running his hand over the 18 ft. Outrigger canoe.

"I'm a modern Vahine." Hinano said proudly. *"I can surf on the Internet, but I keep alive my Tahitian culture and traditions."*

"When Mama gave me this va'a, she told me her Father built it from a hollowed-out breadfruit tree as a birthday gift when she was a tamahini to go fishing on the lagoon."

"Every six months, I restore it using the same methods and materials used by our ancestors."

"Now it's my turn to paddle you on the reef and discover its secrets with me."

"You paddle in front and navigate us through the coral gardens until we reach the channel behind the reef crown." Hinano said, pushing her va'a off the beach, and with the first powerful stroke of her paddle, thrust the outrigger canoe gliding across the turquoise lagoon.

17 ... Love at First Sight

"This is the most fun I've had with you since I came to Tahiti!"

"This is your first time on my reef." She giggled, trying to be serious while Isaiah tried to kiss her mangos, bobbing in the wave surge.

"Look where you put your hands and feet."

"There may be a puhi iari / moray eel hiding in the coral waiting to bite your hands or feet."

"Nohu / stone fish with enough deadly cobra-like venom in their dorsal spines that can kill you."

"Any more dangers I should look out for?" He asked, looking up from his mango tasting.

"Yes!" She laughed pushing him back off balance. *"Don't sit on those vana / sea urchins behind you!"*

"Aaugh!" He cried out frantically swimming away from an army of sea urchins waving their 6-inch needle-like spines at his popa'a'a/ white butt. *"Don't scare me like that!"*

"Stay close to me, and I'll teach you the secrets of our coral reefs ."

"The water in your lagoon is crystal clear."
Isaiah called out, admiring the myriad of tropical fish darting under the va'a into the labyrinth of massive coral heads blooming like a vast coral garden in the turquoise lagoon.

His attention focused on Hinano's black silky hair blowing in the trade winds, her brown eyes ablaze with each stroke of her paddle, recalled memories of his Great Grandfather's oil paintings of Hinareva that enchanted generations of his family on Nantucket Island.

The sudden **Thud!** of the solid breadfruit tree hull striking a coral head, sending Isaiah head over heels into the lagoon!

"Let that be a good lesson! Ensign Puckett."
She laughed, helping him climb back into the canoe.
"Stop dreaming and pay attention to paddling us safely to the reef."

"Push my va'a off the coral head." She scolded, pointing the way with her paddle.

"Start paddling, and I will steer us through the coral field until we glide into the into the calm water behind the reef."

Hinano dropped her lava rock anchor into a fault in the reef channel, stepped on a mushroom shaped coral head, and dove into the next wave cascading off the reef crown.

89

17 ... Love at first sight

"You're the most intelligent, hard-working, Vahine I've ever met!" Isaiah said, floating her into his arms while he posed the question every woman wants from the one man she wants to share her love and life.

"Hinano Tamatoa Puckett!" Isaiah said, looking into her dark brown eyes. *"Will you marry me and become my beloved wife."*

"Yes! Isaiah Puckett." Hinano whispered blinking away a flood of happy tears. *"I will marry you and become your beloved wife."*

"Listen to the music of the waves breaking on the reef!" Isaiah sang waltzing Hinano in the sea.

"Will you dance with me to celebrate our engagement?"

"This is more fun than disco dancing!" She said happily. *"I don't have to wear a fancy dress, makeup, or high heel shoes."*

"This is the happiest day of my life!" Isaiah shouted into the trade winds.

"Shall we continue our dance?" She asked, wrapping her legs around him in a lover's embrace.

"I can dance all day with you." He whispered, beginning a slow, intimate waltz in the sea.

"First, take off my bikini." She giggled pushing his shorts around his ankles with her big toe. *"And drop it in my va'a."*

"Are you sure?" Isaiah asked looking into her eyes. *"I can wait until we are married."*

"I'm ready now!" She giggled.

"What about your Tahitian 'Tabu' of no sex on the beach?" Isaiah asked, looking across the lagoon at the tamarii / children playing on the beach.

"We can see them, but they can't see us."

"Is this more of your tahu'a magic?"

"The midday heat waves near the reef destroy our image. We're invisible to them!"

"Sex on the beach is Tabu." She giggled. *"Sex out here in the lagoon is our 'National Sport!"*

Isaiah paused a moment to reflect on this new Tahitian custom, swept her up in his arms, slipped off her bikini, his shorts, and tossed them into her va'a.

"Be gentle with me!" She whispered. *"I'm a vahine api / a virgin!"*

*****

18 ... Even their va'a is invisible

Mama sat in the shade of a purau tree, scanning the reef with her late husband's fishing binoculars.

"Do you see them?" Her Cousin Tara asked.

"The sun is hot today." Mama said, putting away her binoculars. "The heat waves near the reef are powerful. Even their va'a is invisible."

"They will be paddling home soon hungry and sunburned."

"Look!" Tara said. "Hinano left behind her fishing pole."

"Many a young Tane came here to court Hinano," Mama said looking across the lagoon. "When she showed no interest, they left and never came back."

"Until the day she brought home, Isaiah searching for his family's roots."

"When he realized she was fa'a'amu/ adopted, they looked at each other for a long moment, and I could see it was love at first sight!"

"It was then that I knew Hinano was saving herself for the one Tane who would win her heart, mind, body, and soul."

Mama double winked her eyebrows at her Cousin.

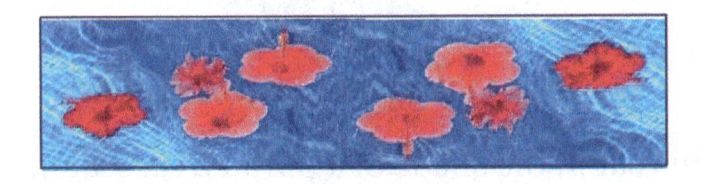

"The golden purau / hibiscus flowers are falling in the lagoon. It's time for me to go home."

"They will be paddling home soon, hungry, tired, and sunburned!" Mama said, watching the sunset behind the reef.

"Be sure and let me know if Hinano catches her Prince Charming!" Tara laughed waving parahi / farewell and began walking home along the beach, carrying her string of orange and green parrotfish. "Or throws him back as too small!"

*****

19 ... An Old Tahitian Love Song

"This has been the most extraordinary day of my life!" Isaiah said looking at the hundreds of golden hibiscus flowers floating across the lagoon.

"I've asked for your hand in marriage, and we've been making love in the sea for hours."
"I'm sunburned, tired, and hungry."

"Plup!!" Hinano giggled crucking her finger.
"It's time to go home. You need a cold shower and a hearty meal."

"Before we go to bed, I'll treat your sunburn with Tahitian medicine."

"Tomorrow morning after breakfast we'll paddle out here behind the reef and make love in the sea all day." She said, watching her new Tane lift his naked body into the va'a and sit down on the hot seat.

"Ouch!" He shouted, jumping to his feet.

"Wrap my wet pareo around your sunburned butt." She laughed splashing fresh seawater on the hot seat, hauled in the stone anchor, picked up her paddle, and turned the va'a towards the beach.

"Are you ready, my love?" He asked, picking up his paddle.

"Hoe te va'a/ paddle the canoe." She said, dipping her paddle into the sea and matching his powerful strokes; they paddled across the lagoon, to their destiny and future.

"When I'm happy, I like to sing!" Hinano called, paddling across the lagoon covered with thousands of golden hibiscus flowers. *"Will you sing along with me?"*

"We'll begin with an old Tahitian love song." "I'll sing the 1st lines; then you join me."

"Hoe, Piti, Toru! / One, Two, Three"

"Vini, Vini, Vini! Vana, Vana, Vana! Te Vahine Tahiti!"

"Vini, Vini, Vini! Vana, Vana, Vana! Te Vahine Tahiti!"

"Now, let's sing together!" Hinano laughed drumming the musical beat with her hands on the outrigger canoe.

"Vini, Vini, Vini! Vana, Vana, Vana! Te Vahine Tahiti!"

"Vini, Vini, Vini! Vana, Vana, Vana! Te Vahine Tahiti!"

"To Tino, To Tino, Te Vahine Tahiti! Ta Ratou Ma'u"

"Peu! Rii'e Tu Ra O Te Aue Tu'na o'te Au'e!"

A Vahine Ruau / Old Woman cleaning a string of parrotfish at the water's edge looked up at two dark silhouettes paddling across the lagoon singing the old Tahitian love song brought back a flood of happy memories from her youth when she paddled home from the reef with her first Tane.

The last orange and violet rays of sunset streaked across the coral reef when Isaiah and Hinano rolled the va'a into her 'Secret Spot' under the purau tree.

"I will always love you from the bottom of my heart!" He said, taking his Vahine in a lover's embrace.

"Ua here vau ia oe! / And I will always love you!" She whispered, wiping away his tears of joy.

On a white sand beach covered with golden hibiscus flowers, two lovers kissed, pausing only to watch two snow-white fairy terns …

… alight on a high branch for the night and dream a lovers' dream.

20 ... Mama's Blessing

"Did you have a nice day on the reef?" Mama asked Hinano leading Isaiah up the stairs onto the veranda.

"We had a wonderful day!" She called out, beaming her radiant smile.

"What happened to him?" Mama asked, looking at the tired, sunburned young American standing on the veranda holding Hinano's hand.

"It was his 1st time on our reef." Hinano laughed, holding up his shorts like a prized trophy. *"He sunburned his butt!"*

"You both need a cold shower." Mama said smiling at her Granddaughter.

"Dinner will be ready in 30 minutes."

"I brought home some take out Chinese food from Papeete. Chow mein, mandarin duck, and nems in a ginger sauce."

"I'm hungry as a grizzly bear after a long hibernation." Isaiah growled following Hinano into the cold shower.

Ten minutes later, Hinano pranced into the dining room wearing a bright orange and yellow pareo, drying her hair with a beach towel, and combing out her tangles with a plastic comb copied from an ancient model made from a Hawksbill turtle shell.

"You look like a boiled lobster!" Mama said, grinning at Isaiah walking painfully into the dining room wearing a bright red pareo over his sunburned butt.

"Today Isaiah asked me to become his beloved wife!" Hinano said happily.

"What was your response?" Mama asked.

"Yes! I will marry him and become his beloved wife!"

"I'm very happy for you!" Mama said taking her place at the head of the table.

"I'll make a prayer to ask God's blessing on your marriage engagement."

Hinano and Isaiah held hands and bowed their heads while Mama closed her eyes and began her prayer.

"I ask God's blessing on Isaiah and Hinano, who have decided to spend their lives together, create a family, and pass on their heritage to their children. Amen."

"Thank you for your prayers and blessing!" Isaiah whispered at Mama, wiping away her tears of joy while Hinano took her Grandmother in a warm embrace.

"Tamaa maitai! / Eat well!" Mama said, picking up a won ton with her chopsticks.

"Your Chinese food is delicious." Isaiah said, learning the art of eating with chopsticks.

"Hinano is famous for her Chinese cuisine." Mama said of her Granddaughters' culinary skills. "Everyone compliments her kai fan, fried rice with pork, and mandarin duck."

"I'm part Chinese from my Father's side." Hinano said, smiling at her Tane. "When I go to visit my family in Bora Bora. He gives me lessons in the art of Chinese wok cuisine."

"What other flavors do you come in?" Isaiah asked.

"Italian from my Mother's side. My pasta, pizzas with lots of tomato sauce, mozzarella cheese, and olive oil are popular with my family and friends." Hinano said recounting her Italian culinary skills.

"Once a year when my Uncle Teiki and his family come from Nuku Hiva to visit Mama Puckett, his wife Tahia teaches me her Marquesan cuisine."

"She has many recipes for wild horses and goats brought to the Marquesas Islands by the Spanish."

"I didn't know we had Puckett family living in the Marquesas Islands?"

"In 1859 Hinareva's Son, Toma Puckett, a handsome young adventurer in his early 20's sailed to the Marquesas Islands to work for an English trading company on Nuku Hiva logging rare tropical hardwoods from the islands primal forests." Mama said, recounting another facet in her family history.

"To decorate their naked bodies, they invented a body art we call tattoo."

"Toma had himself tattooed from head to barefoot with the finest Marquesan body art."

"He quickly became very popular with the local Vahines who came to admire his tattooed muscles."

"The missionaries who followed the loggers into the remote valleys were met by many Marquesan Vahines carrying Toma's babies in their arms and swollen bellies." She said laughing along with Hinano.

"Toma's amorous adventures led to his early demise before his 26th birthday by a jealous Warrior Chief who caught him with his young Vahine."

"The Marquesan Warrior Chief sold Toma's tanned head, and tattooed skin to a German collector and are on display in a museum in Europe." Mama said concluding another chapter of her family history. "Toma has many descendants living in the Marquesas Islands."

"It's getting late." She said hearing the bronze clock on the wall strike the hour. "Time for me to go to bed. What are your plans for tomorrow?"

"We plan to paddle out on the reef before the sun gets too hot for his sunburned butt." Hinano said beaming him a sexy smile. "We have a full moon, so tomorrow my Tane will have the force of a young toro."

"Come with me." Mama whispered leading Hinano into her bedroom. "I'll give you a bottle of my herbal monoi to massage into his sunburn to ease the inflammation and pain."

"Sit next to me, and let's have a heart to heart talk." She said taking Hinano's hand.

"One of my greatest pleasures in life has been to watch you grow up into an intelligent, hardworking, and beautiful Vahine api / virgin."

"I've seen many young men follow you home to court you. When you showed no interest they left and never returned. Until the day you brought home, Isaiah, in search of his Tahitian family."
"When he called you Cousin Hinano, you became furious at him and me! When I told him you were fa'a'amu/ my adopted Granddaughter, you looked into each other's eyes, and I could see it was love at first sight."

"It was then that I knew you were saving yourself for the one man who would win your heart, mind, body, and soul."

"Yes, Mama. How could you tell?"

"When you pulled that exhausted young American with his sunburned butt up the stairs on the veranda and waved his shorts at me like a prized trophy." She laughed. "You were radiant, and I could see it in your eyes."

"Was he gentle with you?"

"Yes, Mama. I was a Vahine api, and he was very gentle and tender with me." She giggled shyly. "I became a little wild and uncontrollable with him!"

"We had a marvelous time making love in the sea all afternoon."

"I hope you didn't hurt him." Mama laughed.

"No, Mama. When he became fatigued and went **Plup!**" She giggled crooking her finger.

"Before you paddle him out on the reef, have him drink this 'Secret Potion' handed down from our ancestors that works like that blue pill you see advertised on television."
She laughed handing Hinano a small glass flacon.

"Tomorrow morning, paddle him out on the reef and make me another grandchild."

"Did you have a nice talk with your Grandmother?" Isaiah asked, finishing the dishes in the kitchen sink.

"Yes! My love. I have no secrets from her."
"I told her how gentle and virile you were with me."

*****

21 ... Hinano's traditional medicine

"Come with me, and I'll treat your sunburn." Hinano said leading him into a guest room converted into a traditional medicine clinic. *"I'm going outside and collect a few medicinal plants."*
"I'll be back in 15 minutes!"

"We have a full moon tonight." Hinano said looking out the open window. *"The tree sap will be strong and the drug potent."*

"Do you have a black cat?"

"Mino! Mino! Come in here and meet Isaiah."

Suddenly! The biggest black cat Isaiah had ever seen leaped on the window sill, stared suspiciously at Isaiah with glowing emerald green eyes, then jumped down to sniff his bare feet.

"We'll go outside, collect a few medicinal plants, and be back in a few minute." Hinano said, picking up her broom niau, pandanus bag, bush knife, and walked into the night, followed by two glowing green cat's eyes.

Isaiah sat on the treatment table, looking at the full moon shining through the window, waiting for Hinano to fly by on her broom niau waving and laughing at him.

"I'm back!" Hinano whispered, scaring the hell out of him!

Isaiah peered over Hinano's shoulder, watching her take a handful of leaves and roots, meticulously scrub and clean them with pure rainwater, pound them with a black jade penu / pestle into a moist pulp.

 Squeeze and filter the natural extract through a bundle of fibers into a coconut shell to which she stirred a finger of pape ha'ari/ coconut water.

"Drink this." Hinano said, handing Isaiah a coconut shell filled with a brown herbal tea.

"It has a strong woody taste." He said, taking his medicine like a grown-up.

"Did you know 25 % of all prescription drugs have their origin in a natural molecule from a medicinal plant from the tropical regions of the earth?" The Tahua's Apprentice said looking at him.

105

"You can buy a synthetic chemical copy of this natural molecule in a pill at your pharmacy, but we like to use the natural molecule that is more potent."

"My Tahitian patients have more confidence in our natural molecules than synthetic pills and tablets made from fine chemicals."

"I've seen movies about Medicine Men, but this is my first experience with a Tahua Vahine / Medicine Woman."

"Take off your pareo, Mr. Puckett, climb on my treatment table, and lay flat on your stomach." She said examining his hairy bare butt and raw shoulders. "Your shoulders and butt are starting to blister."

"What are you going to do with those long needles?" He asked, warily.

"Acupuncture." She said sticking her steel needles into his ears and toes. "To relieve your headache and pain."

"Now, I'll begin the massage." She said, pouring an herbal monoi lotion into the palms of her hands and smoothing it over Isaiah's sunburn from his neck to his feet.

"That feels great!" Isaiah grunted while she massaged the perfumed Monoi into his aching back, arm, neck, and leg muscles.

Ten minutes later, she paused to wipe the sweat off her brow. "Rollover on your back, and I'll massage the other side."

"Now, I understand why Mama never let me work on a Tane!" Hinano giggled, massaging soothing Monoi lotion into Isaiah's hairy chest, stomach, and leg muscles.

After a few minutes, Isaiah looked up. "Haven't you missed something?"

"No, Mr. Puckett." Hinano scolded him. "This is a medical clinic, not a sex massage parlor!"

"Please check me over to assure my fiancée I'm in good working order."

"Did your Vahine hurt you today?" Dr. Puckett asked, taking him gently in hand for a close inspection.

"It was her first time." Isaiah said enjoying her soothing manipulations. "She got wild and lost control for a few moments, but I think I'm OK!"

"Tell your Vahine to go slow and easy on you tomorrow!" She said gently finishing her task in hand. "How do you feel now?"

"One hundred percent better!"

"You need a good night's sleep, and tomorrow morning after a hearty breakfast you'll feel like a new man."

"I hope so! Tomorrow morning my fiancée and I plan to paddle out on the reef and make love all day in the sea." Isaiah said giving her a 'Thank You' kiss.

"My pain, headache, and soreness are gone."

"Go take a cold shower while I clean up my clinic." She said, handing him a bouquet of fresh-cut gardenias.

"Take these gardenias and put them on the night table to make our bedroom smell nice tonight."

*****

22 ... Ping! Pang! Thud!

Hinano slipped under the mosquito net and wiggled in next to Isaiah's muscular body.

"Humph, our first night in a bed, and my Prince Charming is sound asleep."

"You have beautiful silky hair." Isaiah whispered, caressing her tenderly.

"I thought you were asleep." She giggled, feeling her body tingle when Isaiah caressed her bareback and butt.

"I was resting my eyes while I waited for you." He said softly taking her in a passionate embrace.

"Is it your custom to play your national sport on a bed?"

"You made a rapid recovery." Hinano giggled, feeling her basic instincts take control while her magic touch inflamed his rising passion.

"You got it?" Isaiah whispered, lifting her gently over his muscular thighs.

"Umm! Right where I want it." She whispered, urgently, her instinct and passion rise and fall in perfect rhythm with her lover.

Squeak! Squeak! Squeak!

"Ieee! What's that horrible noise?" Hinano called out into the night.

"The rusty springs on this cast iron bed!" He whispered smiling up at her. *"Don't worry about it! I'll oil them in the morning."*

Ping! Pang! Thud!

"Aeeooh!" Hinano cried out again squeezing him in a vise grip. *"What was that?"*

"I can't be sure until you get off me and let me look." Isaiah laughed, lifting her aside and peering under the bed frame.

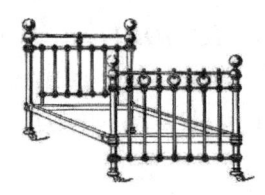

"Wow! You hammered the cast iron bed posts through the rotten floor, broke the springs, and bent the bed frame!"
He laughed inspecting Hinano's artwork. *"Wait until I tell my friends in the Navy!"*

"I'll turn you into a frog if you do!"

"In the morning, we'll get some tools from the workshop and fix the bed." Hinano whispered.

"Before my family sees it and the story goes around the island."

In the moonlight, two emerald-green cat's eyes watched two naked shadows tiptoe across the dining room.

Hinano, "Be quiet and follow me. We'll go sleep in my bedroom."

"What was that loud crash?" Mama called out.

"The bed fell through the rotten floorboards. We'll fix it in the morning. Sleep tight!"

"You too!" She called out, trying to hold back her laughter with a pillow over her head!

Hinano, "I can hear her laughing at us!"

"Show me the way to your bedroom." Isaiah whispered after Hinano tiptoeing across the main salon. "Your nao nao / mosquitoes are feasting on my bare butt."

Hinano climbed in bed next to her Tane, tucked in the mosquito net, and lay her head on his shoulder.

"Look at the magnificent full moon rising over the coral reef." Isaiah said softly, caressing Hinano's sensual curves silhouetted in the silver moonlight.

"Ua here vau ia oe." Hinano whispered, kissing him goodnight.

"I love you too." Isaiah whispered, returning her kiss, fell into a deep sleep, and dreamt a lover's dream.

23 ... Hinareva's fit of jealousy

"Good morning, Mama." Hinano yawned, taking her chair in front of a bowl of strong coffee.

"You and Isaiah had an exciting night." She said, joining her Granddaughter for breakfast.

"A fascinating night!" Hinano said, laughing at the thought.

"I saw the shipwrecked bed." Mama laughed winking her eyes at Hinano. *"I hope you didn't get hurt."*

"No, but it gave me a real fright. We slept in Hinareva's bedroom last night. I could feel her tu'pau'pa'u / ghostly presence." Hinano said worried about Hinareva's fit of jealousy. *"You think she got angry with us for sleeping in her bed and made it collapse?"*

"Young Isaiah certainly does resemble his Great Grandfather." Mama said, trying to explain Hinareva's fit of jealousy. *"Maybe she confused Isaiah with her Tane Capt Puckett."*

"This morning, Isaiah and I will get some tools from the workshop and patch the holes Hinareva's bedroom floor so we can use her bedroom again as a family guestroom."

Hinareva, *"Tonight we'll sleep in my bedroom, and I'll light my tu'pau'pau / ghost lamp."*

"Good Morning, Isaiah!" Mama asked. *"Did you sleep well!"*

Hinano, *"Last night was an adventure!"*

"Try a bowl of Uncle Teiki's gourmet coffee mountain grown on his Puckett Plantation in the Marquesas Islands."

"We're having fried marara fish, taro poi, and boiled fei / bananas for breakfast." She said, filling his plate.

"These fish have wings!" Isaiah said, holding up one by its wings.

"Of course!" Hinano said giving him a puzzled look. *"They are Marara / flying fish."*

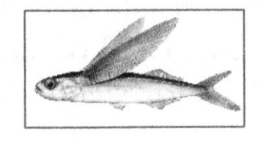

"They're delicious." Isaiah said, pulling off and crunching another fish wing. *"We slept late this morning. It's almost 10 am."*

"Why don't we fix the shipwrecked bed this morning and paddle on the reef this afternoon when it's cooler." Isaiah said, biting off a crunchy Marara fish head and stripping out the tasty meat with his fingers.

*****

24 ... The Plantation Workshop

"Watch your step!" Hinano said leading Isaiah into the thicket of purau trees. *"Our Plantation Workshop is 100 feet behind the beach."*

A few minutes later, she stopped in front of a crumbling coral and lava rock ruin overgrown with 20 years of purau roots and green vines barely holding up the rusty tin roof. Hinano watched Isaiah's eyes widen in surprise while he studied the crumbling workshop hidden away in the hibiscus thicket.

"My Great Grandfather and his Nantucket whalers built this workshop in 1840." He said recounting the history learned at his Father's feet in front of a blazing driftwood fireplace during a long winter's night.

"Look at this blacksmith's forge, anvil, and drop the hammer the whalers used to make the first wrought iron tools, nails, bolts, and horseshoes in Tahiti." He said, climbing through the tangle of green vines and roots growing over the crumbling ruin.

*"Here the **Molly Puckett's** Ship's Carpenter set up the first sawmill to cut rough trees into squared posts, beams, and boards to construct his plantation home; strong enough to resist the fierce tropical cyclones that devastated Tahiti and her Islands every few years."*

"His whalemen taught the Tahitians fine carpentry to build finely crafted tables, beds, chairs, and furniture for their new anticyclone plantation homes."

"In this workshop, the Nantucket whalers and the Tahitians built the first sailing schooners to trade between Moorea, the British Society Islands, and the Tuamotu Atolls."

"We used this workshop until Mama's husband Manu died, and their Sons abandoned the plantation." Hinano said, pointing to a vine covered one cylinder diesel generator set, rusted fuel tanks, and power relay cables dangling off the crumbling coral and lava rock wall.

"This old English diesel generator set provided electricity for our Puckett Plantation for almost half a century."

"After we're married, I'm going to invite my father to return with us to Tahiti, and we'll rebuild Mama's plantation home and workshop. We'll buy a new farm tractor and chainsaw to clear the overgrown coconut plantation and orange grove."

"Wow! This must be the 1939 Ford pickup truck Mama and her husband Manu bought in San Francisco?" Isaiah said, clearing off a tangle of vines and shooing away a pair of jungle fowl nesting on the front seat.

"My Dad always dreamed of restoring one of these antique Ford trucks."

"Looks like it needs an oil change, a tune up, four new tires, and a fresh coat of black paint." He said, making a quick walk-around inspection. "My Dad and I will restore this classic pickup and take our family on a circle island tour of Tahiti and Moorea."

"That'll be great fun!" Hinano said, holding Isaiah's hand while they explored the crumbling ruin.

"Did you find some tools to fix the shipwrecked bed?" She asked Isaiah rummaging through the toolboxes and parts bins.

"I found a sledgehammer to straighten out the wrought iron bed frame."

"I'll need this blacksmith's tool to straighten out the bed frame, a roll of baling wire to repair the broken springs, and shortboards to patch over the holes in the floor."

"I'm ready to go back when you are."

"We'll go back in a few minutes." Hinano said rummaging around in a dusty tool chest.
"I have something for you."

"Here it is!" She said gently lifting out a long metal object wrapped in waxed canvas sailcloth.

Hinano, "Do you remember the color photos you brought with you from America?"

"Robert Pratt's oil painting of Capt Puckett and Hinareva standing on the veranda of our plantation home in 1842?"

"I remember Hinareva wearing an ankle length red velvet dress typical of the 1800s." He recalled. "She wore tiare / Tahiti flowers in her hair."

"A whale ivory and pearl necklace showing her rank as the daughter of a Arii / High Chief."

"What was your Great Grandfather wearing?" She asked, teasing his memory.

"His broad-brimmed whaling master's hat, a bristling black beard, and a serious expression on his face typical of his era."

"A dark blue greatcoat with shiny brass buttons and a wide leather belt with a brass buckle held up his black pants tucked into knee-high leather boots."

"When you told me how he fought against King George's Royal Navy with a pistol and cutlass. I remembered this."

"Capt Puckett's cutlass!" Isaiah called out picking up the hand-forged steel, and brass handled weapon; and reading the inscription engraved on the hilt.

Capt Isaiah Puckett
Who dares! Wins!

"When I was a tamahine / little girl, I found Capt Puckett's cutlass hidden in this chest. "

"When Mama caught me playing pirate with my cousins in her va'a, she got angry and spanked me with her broom niau for playing with this dangerous tipi / long knife."

"When I was 16 years old, my uncles taught me how to use this tipi / long knife to kill pigs, goats, and cattle to store in our freezer and cook in our ground oven."

"I realized this cutlass was a dangerous weapon to butcher long two legged pigs and short four legged pigs!"

"This short-bladed cutlass was developed by English and American pirates as a close combat weapon to board and seize Spanish galleons carrying stolen Inca gold to Spain during the 1500s."

He said recounting the cutlasses bloody history. "Many pirates took up their cutlasses to join our fledgling United States Navy, and fought against King George's Royal Navy during our 1st War for Independence in 1776 and again during the 2nd War of 1812."

"French pirate Capt Jean Lafitte and 1000 pirates joined American General Andrew Jackson's 6500 soldiers in soundly defeating King George's force of 7500 led by General Edward Pakenham in the epoch 1815 Battle of New Orleans."

"Capt Puckett's fearless reputation in a battle against his enemies made his officers and crew; fear and respect him at all times."

"When faced with a potential mutiny Capt Puckett port his Father's cutlass as a warning, he would defend his ship and command to his death."

"He always accomplished his mission and sailed his ship safely back to her Home Port." Isaiah said smiling at Hinano. "His courage and leadership in battle have inspired generations of descendants who followed him."

"You're very proud of him." She said softly.

"I'm proud to carry his name!"

"This cutlass has been in our custody for over 160 years," Hinano said, handing him the ancient pirate's weapon. "I'm sure Capt Puckett is pleased I return it to his Great Grandson, Ensign Isaiah Puckett II, of the US Navy, to defend his family, his ship, and country against all enemies."

"Thank you! Hinano." Isaiah said picking up his tools, oil can, sharpening stone, and a wire brush to remove the rust off the cutlass blade and green oxide off the brass handle and hilt. "I will bear this ancient arm with courage and honor."

"When you return to Hawaii, mail me some photos in your dress white navy uniform wearing your cutlass I can show my friends and family my handsome American fiancée."

25 ... A Rising Storm

"It's starting to rain!" Isaiah called out feeling the 1st drops of liquid sunshine falling on his head through the pinholes in the rusty tin roof.

"Let's go back and repair the wrecked bed before Mama returns from Papeete."

It was late afternoon and pouring rain when Mama hurried up the stairs, handed her umbrella, and shopping bag to Hinano waiting on the veranda with a dry towel.

*"Did you have a busy day in **Papeete's Public Market**?"*

"On **Cruise Ship Day**, hundreds of tourists come shopping for a flower lei, taste our tropical fruits, and take home a nice gift or handicraft made in Tahiti from the Tahitian Mamas who sell directly to them at reasonable prices." Mama said, smiling at Isaiah. "I sold many tiare Tahiti / flower leis to several American families. Everyone was surprised I could speak English."

"I sold many tiare Tahiti / flower leis to several American families. Everyone was surprised I could speak English."

"This morning we had 100's of happy tourists off a cruise ship shopping in the market."

"Today's best sellers were vanilla beans and mother of pearl jewelry." She said with a twinkle in her eye.

"This morning, a Tahitian dance group entertained the tourists with their songs, dances, ukuleles, drums, and guitars. Everyone had a great time!"

"After the tourists went back to their cruise ship, I went into the Chinese Quarter and bought some 'take out' food for our dinner."

"I bought a piece of mahi-mahi, taro, and lychees for our dinner tonight." Mama said, watching Hinano sit down next to Isaiah and begin needlework on her patchwork quilt while he honed his cutlass to a razor's edge.

"Whoosh! Boom! Bam! Bam! Thud!"

"Wow!" Isaiah called out looking up at the rusty tin roof. "That was a strong wind gust!"

"Go check if the coconuts that fell on the roof damaged my potted flowers next to the house?" Hinano asked Isaiah looking out the window at the rising wind gusts and sheets of rain blowing through the overgrown coconut plantation.

"Your flowers are fine!" Isaiah shouted watching the leafy banana plants twisting violently in the rising storm. *"There are a few coconuts and palm fronds on the ground next to the house."*

"What a great day for your ducks!" He laughed, watching a dozen white ducks marching single file from under the house flapping their wings and quacking happily in the pouring rain.

"The weather report this morning forecast a small tropical depression hitting us from the northeast." Hinano said putting aside her needlework.
"We may be in for some stormy weather for the next few days."

"Let's go move my va'a off the beach before the storm hits hard." Hinano shouted, tossing Isaiah a foul weather jacket. Together they ran into the rising storm, leaping over downed banana plants and coconut leaves, into the storm surge, and seafoam rising on the beach.

"Help me push my va'a on the coconut log rollers under the workshop!" She shouted at Isaiah wiping the wind-driven salt spray sandblasting his face. "Let's roll!"

Isaiah put his shoulder against the outrigger canoe and pushed while Hinano placed the coconut log rollers one after the other until the va'a was safely in the workshop.

"Let's hurry back to the house, batten down the storm shutters, and get ready for the storm!" Hinano shouted over her shoulder leading him through the narrow bush track littered with fallen limbs and downed banana plants.

Mama stood on the veranda watching Hinano and Isaiah bounding up the lava rock and coral stairs.

"The va'a is safely in the workshop!" Hinano shouted removing her foul weather jacket. *"Help me close the storm louvers and cover the lounge chairs."*

"Would you like some hot coffee when you finish?"

"Yes, Mama." Hinano and Isaiah shouted in unison.

"A small tropical depression is moving this way." Isaiah tapping the bronze ships barometer hanging on the wall. *"The needle dropped 2 points."*

"Tonight we'll look at the weather report and satellite photo on television and see if it's a passing tropical depression or an early tropical cyclone." She said drying her hair with a towel and enjoying a hot cup of coffee with Mama and Isaiah.
"This is the first tropical depression of the year!"
"We need the rain for our flower garden."

"When it rains it pours!" Isaiah said surprised by a sudden splash of rainwater falling on his head.

"Whoosh! Boom! Plok! Plok! Plok!"

"Whoops! There goes another bunch of coconuts on the roof!" Isaiah shouted looking at the drops of water falling on the floor. "Your tin roof leaks like a sieve."

"Yes, Yes, like a sieve." Mama laughed.

Isaiah looked up at the rainwater pouring through the holes in the rusty tin roof. "When was the last time you nailed new tin roofing on this old plantation house?"

Mama scratched her gray hair and thought for a moment. "Manu and my Sons nailed on a new tin roof about 30 years ago."

"My Dad always dreamed of flying to Tahiti to find his Tahitian Puckett family, but he got caught up in the Vietnam War." He called out to Mama and Hinano rushing around the house placing red plastic buckets under the rainwater streaming through the holes in their rusty tin roof.

"I'm sure he would love to come to Tahiti to visit with his wonderful Cousin Mama Puckett and her family."

"When I return to Tahiti, I'll bring my Dad to help repair our Great Grandfather's home."

"The first thing we'll do is nail new tin roofing on this old house and workshop, replace the rotten floor, and install a solar water heater on the roof so we can enjoy a hot shower."

"Why don't you telephone him and I'll invite him!" Mama said to a stunned Isaiah. "What's his telephone number?"

"What a great idea!" Isaiah said looking at his watch and calculating the time zone difference.

"He's likely working late tonight. Let me dial for you."

"Puckett Boat Shop." A deep male voice answered.

"I would like to speak to Joshua Puckett?"

"This is Joshua Puckett."

"I'm your Grandmother Ahu'ura Puckett calling from Tahiti."

There was no response, only a long silence!

"Do you understand my English? Joshua Puckett." She demanded.

"Yes, I understand you perfectly." Joshua whistled under his breath.

"When Isaiah arrived in search of his Tahitian family, it was a total surprise and shock for us too." Mama said, laughing at him.

"It was you, Dad, who challenged Jonah and me to fly to Tahiti and find our Tahitian family roots and heritage Capt Puckett and Hinareva left for us." He said recounting his adventure searching for his family's roots.

"I found Mama and her adopted granddaughter Hinano living in an old plantation home built in 1840 by our Great Grandfather on what is now called the 'Puckett Plantation."

"After I recounted our family history, Mama took me to their family cemetery where she had me dig up a headstone that had fallen over and was lying face down covered with soil and grass for over a century."

"We cleaned off the headstone and read the epitaph inscribed by our Great Grandfather."

Here lies Hinareva Puckett
Beloved wife of Isaiah Puckett

"It matches the epitaph on Capt Puckett's headstone in our family cemetery."

"Mama gave me our Great Grandfather's sextant, with his name Capt Isaiah Puckett, US Navy 1812 engraved on the walnut case."

"Hinano gave me his pirate's cutlass she found in their plantation workshop you will immediately recognize as a copy of our Puckett Boat Shop."

"The overgrown workshop has Capt Puckett's blacksmith forge, drop hammer, whaling harpoons, flaying knives, and a cauldron used to boil down whale blubber that came off his whaling ship."

"The physical evidence, Mama's oral history, and genealogy fill in many holes in our family history." Isaiah concluded.

"I found our Tahitian Puckett family and our Great Grandfather's heritage!"

"I've always dreamed of flying to Tahiti," Joshua said.

"I'm delighted to accept Mama's invitation to visit our Tahitian family!"

"When you come, I have a gift for you and Isaiah." Mama said taking the telephone away from Isaiah.

"Something Isaiah said you always dreamed of owning. A 1940 Ford pickup truck my Tane and I bought in San Francisco. After he died, I parked it in our workshop."

"Isaiah thinks it needs a tune-up, oil, grease, new tires, and a fresh coat of black paint."

She said happily recalling the days before Tahiti had paved roads and freeways with 25,000 cars, trucks, and scooters racing in a mad frenzy every day around the Island at 100 km per hour.

"If you and Isaiah can make my old pickup run again. I would love to drive you around the Island of Tahiti."

"I have another surprise for you, Dad." Isaiah said taking back the telephone. "I've met the woman of my dreams. Her name is Hinano Tamatoa Puckett."

"I'm not his Cousin!" Hinano shouted over his shoulder.

"I heard that!" Joshua said, laughing at her remark.

"Hinano was faa' mu / adopted from the Tamatoa family on the Island of Bora Bora and raised by Mama Puckett."

"She is the most intelligent, hard-working, loving, beautiful, and sexy woman I've ever met."

"I've asked her to marry me and become my beloved wife!"

"Now that's a real surprise!" Joshua laughed.

"Wait until you meet her, Dad. She's terrific."

"I'm right here, Papa Puckett." Hinano shouted, grabbing the telephone from Isaiah.

"I'm happy to meet you! Everyone calls me Joshua."

"That's not our Tahitian custom. It's not polite!"

"When Isaiah asked me to become his wife."
She said with impeccable Tahitian logic.

"It's our custom when I become your daughter-in-law I must call you Papa Puckett."

"I'm honored if you call me Papa Puckett!"

"What are your marriage plans?"

"Isaiah wants to get married in your home by your American marriage rites on Nantucket Island and return to Tahiti for traditional Polynesian marriage by our Tahitian rites with a tama'ara'a/feast on our Pucket Plantation."

"But first he wants to quit his job in the US Navy. I need time off from my job as a schoolteacher.

We have to work this out before we get married and set our course in life as husband and wife."

"I read your registered letter from Hawaii. Cmdr Hoffman was a bad experience for a young junior officer beginning his first tour of duty in the Navy."

"I understand your decision to resign from the Navy and get on with your life."

"Thank you, Dad. For your support."

"Tomorrow I'll email you my digital photos of Mama, Hinano, and their Puckett Plantation."

"Are you still planning to go to the Marquesas?"

"Yes, I plan to book passage aboard an inter-island freighter and depart for the Marquesas Islands in a few days."

"We have a developing tropical depression so it all depends on the weather."

"I'll try to call you when I arrive there. I'll say 'Goodbye' for now! Dad."

"Parahi! Everybody." Joshua said, saying farewell.

"Parahi! / Bye-bye! Papa Puckett." Hinano shouted over Isaiah's shoulder.

"Parahi / Farewell, my young Cousin from Nantucket Island." Mama laughed, ending the telephone call to America.

"Tell us your mysterious plans to go to the Marquesas?" Hinano asked curiously.

"I'm working on my Master's Degree in Marine Science through a University Advanced Degree Program offered to armed forces personnel who want to pursue their Master or Phd. Degree."

Hinano, "You want to become Dr. Isaiah Puckett, a famous marine scientist?"

"I plan to go to the Northern Marquesas Islands and do a 1-kilometer survey of the marine biosystem for my Master's Degree thesis."

"The Marquesas like the Hawaiian Islands are volcanic in origin and have similar tropical marine biosystems."

"I brought several scientific instruments for this marine research project." Isaiah said, beaming the two Puckett Vahines a confident smile.

"I should be able to complete my marine survey in two weeks, and return before the end of my 30 days leave."

"Do you plan on going alone?" Hinano asked curiously.

"Yes!" Isaiah said, beaming her another confident smile.

"Humph!" Hinano remarked, disappointed at his reply.

"Why don't you telephone the Interisland Freighter Office in the Port of Papeete to book your passage." She said, returning to the veranda.

A few minutes later, Isaiah returned with disappointment on his face. "I telephoned three inter island companies serving the Marquesas. They are booked solid for the next two months."

"Why don't you try 'Air Manuroa?" Hinano suggested.

Five minutes later, Hinano and Mama Puckett watched Isaiah put down the telephone, walk out on the veranda, flop down on the couch, and stare into the wind gusts and rain blowing through the coconut trees.

"What happened?" She asked her very troubled Tane.

"All Air Manuroa flights to the Marquesas are reserved for the next four weeks."

"I only have 30 days leave." Isaiah said bitterly. "I have no choice but to give up my marine science project in the Marquesas."

"Why don't you ask Hinano to help you?" Mama whispered into Isaiah's ear, making him think for a moment.

Hinano, "Show me on a map of the Marquesas exactly where you want to go and exactly what you want to do when we get there."

"We?" Isaiah asked.

"Yes! Hinano and Isaiah Puckett until death do us part." Hinano said, beaming him another radiant smile.

"It's wild and maybe dangerous in the Marquesas."

"Yes, dangerous for you!" Hinano glared at him. "You can't paddle a va'a without going on the first coral head. These are my islands and my people."

"I speak the language and can survive in the Marquesas. I'm not so sure about you."

"Now make your decision. Return to Hawaii alone, or we go together to the Marquesas!"

"I have no choice?" He asked, looking at the two Vahines, shaking their heads at him.

A few minutes later, Isaiah returned from his bedroom, set his notebook computer on the dining room table, clicked down a satellite photo of the Pacific Ocean, until a close-up image of Tahiti zoomed on the screen.

"There's Tahiti-Faaa Airport and Papeete!" Hinano said looking over his shoulder as Isaiah zoomed on their Puckett Plantation. *"Look, Mama, there's your home, garden, and the beach."*

Isaiah zoomed closer until he focused on a Vahine in a string bikini sunbathing on the beach, fronting their home.

"That's Hinano's friend Tetua!" Mama said.

"Where did you get these satellite photos?" Hinano asked.

"They were taken a month ago from the ISS / International Space Station." Isaiah double-clicked again displaying a satellite photo of Nuku Hiva in the Marquesas and five small islands in the Northern Group. He continued zooming on the smaller islands following the rugged cliffs and valleys until he stopped his pointer in front of a flat-topped volcanic cone. *"This is where I want to do my scientific survey. It looks dangerous, with oceanic swells rising, and crashing directly on the cliffs."*

"Show me how to run this imaging program." Hinano asked, pushing him aside and zooming along Nuku Hiva's bays and rugged valleys.

"Uncle Teiki and his family live in this remote valley!" She said, finishing her satellite recon.

"I have several telephone calls to make, and I'll be back in a few minutes."

Hinano completed her 1st telephone call and signaled her Grandmother to turn up the volume on the radio. Suddenly her voice came booming over **'Radio Tahiti'**!

"What's Hinano doing on 'Radio Tahiti'?" Isaiah asked.

"She is sending a personal message in Marquesan to her Cousin Teiki living in a remote valley on the island of Nuku Hiva."

"The only contact Teiki and his family have with the outside world is a shortwave radio."

"They listen to 'Radio Tahiti' for news, weather, and personal messages from their families."

"Here it comes." Mama said, translating Hinano's message into English.

"Message for Teiki Puckett and family on Nuku Hiva! Arrive by Air Manuroa at noon tomorrow.

Hinano and Isaiah Puckett from Paea, Tahiti."

"Come, Mama." Hinano said taking her by the hand down the stairs to the pickup truck parked under the breadfruit tree.
"Let's go shopping in Papeete for a few gifts we'll bring with us to Uncle Teiki's family."

It was close to midnight when Hinano and Isaiah finished packing their airline bags, luggage, cartons and set them on the veranda.

Hinano lit up an ancient whale oil lamp and led him into her bedroom.

"Do you think this tropical storm will get stronger tonight?" He asked, watching Hinano place a hurricane lamp on the night table next to her bed and turn up the flame until a bright orange glow filled her bedroom.

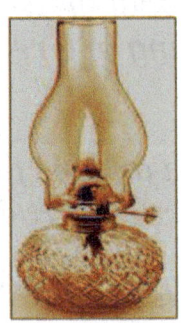

"The lamp is to keep away Hinareva's tu'pau' pau / ghost. Last night, I could feel her presence in her bedroom. Sometimes, our ancestors' ghosts come into our homes at night."
She whispered taking comfort in his warm embrace.
"We can feel their presence, or they visit us in our dreams."

"When the tu'pau'pau gets angry, they try to scare us, so we light the ghost lamp to keep them away."

"You do look like your Great Grandfather in the paintings. Maybe your resemblance to her Tane made her jealous."

"Do you have many ghosts on Nantucket Island?"

"Only on Halloween!" Isaiah laughed, taking his Tahitian sorceress in his arms. "Our American Ghost Festival!"

"Do you think if I place a few photos of Capt Puckett and his family on her pillow, she'll be happy?" He asked, sitting on the edge of Hinano's bed.

"That's a good idea." She said, watching him lift a few color prints from his flight bag and carry them into Hinareva's bedroom.

"I put them on Hinareva's pillow." Isaiah whispered returning from his ghost pacification mission. "Now, can I turn off your tu'pau'pau lamp?"

"Yes!" Hinano said snuggling next to her Tane. "Are you happy we are going to the Marquesas together?"

"I'm delighted we're going together." Isaiah said kissing her goodnight. "You were right! "I could never have done it without you."

Hinano, "I've always wanted to go to the Marquesas to visit my Uncle Teiki and his family."

"Ua here vau ia oe." Isaiah whispered, watching the full moon surfing across the Southern Sky on a sea of passing storm clouds.

*****

26 ... An Alcoholic Tyrant!

Cmdr Hoffman took the last swig of Kentucky Bourbon and threw the empty whiskey bottle on the floor of his Navy sedan just in time to see two Navy Shore Patrol jeeps in his rearview mirror flashing red and yellow warning lights.

"I'm well below the 35 mph speed limit." He mumbled, glancing at the blurry image of the speedometer needle.

"Pull over Cmdr Hoffman and turn off your engine!" The Shore Patrol Petty Officer growled over the bullhorn.

"You bastards!" Hoffman snarled, bouncing his navy sedan to a hard stop off the curb.

"Step out of the vehicle, Cmdr Hoffman." The Chief Petty Officer demanded in a polite but firm tone of voice.

"I was well below the speed limit!" He snarled at the Shore Patrolmen, picking up the pile of empty whiskey bottles on the floor, and placing them in a plastic evidence bag.

"Yes, but you were weaving all over the road." The Chief Petty Officer replied firmly. "We want you to take an alcohol breath test."

"Like hell, I will!" Hoffman snarled again, jabbing a quick punch into the Petty Officer's stomach, knocking him to ground.
Two muscular Shore Patrolmen quickly stepped in, forcing Hoffman's face down over the jeep, handcuffing his hands behind his back.

"You OK, Chief?" A 'Voice' from the rear asked.

"Yes! Sir." The Petty Officer said, getting his wind back.

"Stand him up and turn him around so he can see me."

"I'm Capt Alphonse Grieg, Commanding Officer of the Pearl Harbor Shore Patrol."

"I stood next to you at the bar for 2 hours while you set a record for alcohol consumption at Pearl Harbor." Capt Grieg said waving a handful of bar chits in his face. *"Cmdr Roy Hoffman! I order you to take this alcohol breath test."*

Hoffman's hands trembled while he blew into the plastic device, his bloodshot eyes bulging from his bullet-shaped head.

"Give him a 2nd one." Capt Grieg said checking each test vial. *"Cmdr Hoffman, I'm arresting you for drunk driving and assaulting my Chief Petty Officer."*
"Take him away and lock him in the brig!"

Hoffman fell to his knees in a drunken stupor, and began to vomit and defecate over himself while the harsh reality his fate sank slowly into his alcohol drugged brain.

Capt Al Grieg walked over to his jeep and looked at Sgt Major Pete Lopez watching two Shore Patrolmen shove Hoffman into the metal cage on their vehicle and drive off towards the Navy Stockade.

"I'll lock him in the drunk tank for 24 hours until he sobers up. Cmdr. Hoffman's career came to a dead-end tonight. Are you satisfied? Sgt. Major."

"Yes, Sir, for the good of the Navy."

"I'll drop you off at the NIC / Naval Intelligence Center." Capt Grieg said, starting his jeep and speeding off into the Hawaiian night.

It was after midnight when he stopped at the Naval Intelligence Center. *"Tell Adm Porche to order a replacement for Hoffman."*

"I will." Sgt. Major Lopez said. *"Thanks for the ride."*

Sgt. Major Lopez walked towards a silhouette standing in the shadows he immediately recognized as his boss Rear Admiral Charles Porche, Director of the Pearl Harbor NIC / Naval Intelligence Center.

"How did it go with Cmdr Hoffman tonight?"

"Like we planned, Admiral." Sgt. Major Lopez said with a tone of satisfaction.

"Well done, Sgt Major, I telephoned Adm Bill Hansen requesting an urgent meeting tonight to discuss Hoffman's arrest."

"Whenever a field grade officer is arrested by the Shore Patrol's Commanding Officer, he immediately notifies the Commander in Chief Pacific Area Command HQ."

"Adm Hansen likes to do his paperwork at night when there's less interference from his staff."

"Once we get him out of his office we'll have his undivided attention until we finish our 'Top Secret Briefing."

"Is the motor launch and crew ready for our visit tonight?"

"Yes, Sir." Sgt. Major Lopez affirmed. "They're in place and ready to go."

"Let's take your jeep and enjoy this cool Hawaiian night air." Adm Porche said, sitting next to Sgt. Major Lopez, driving slowly along the quays where 100's of sailors and civilian dock workers labored day and night to resupply, refuel, and rearm the US Pacific Fleet's guided-missile cruisers, air craft carriers, nuclear submarines, and supply ships making the United States Navy the dominant naval power in the Pacific Ocean.

*****

27 ... CINCPAC Headquarters

Adm Porche and Sgt. Major Lopez marched briskly up the stairs past the Marine guard to the 'Night Duty Officer.'

"Adm Hansen finished his paperwork and was about to go to his quarters when he received your phone call."

"Please be brief with him. Tomorrow the Admiral has a busy day. A meeting at 0700 with his 7th Fleet Admirals, lunch with several Congressmen from the Senate Armed Services Committee, and a round of golf with Hawaii's Governor."

"We'll do our best to get the Admiral home early." Sgt. Major Lopez said, glaring at the Night Duty Officer.

The Navy Captain double-clicked the CINCPAC icon and looked into the tired face of Adm Bill Hansen.

"Adm Porche and Sgt. Major Lopez to see you."

"Send them in." Adm Hansen said returning their hand salutes. "Good evening, gentlemen! Please come in and take a chair."

"Would you guys like a cup of hot coffee?"

"Thank you, Admiral." The late-night Intruders said, taking a sip of Adm Hansen's gourmet Kona coffee grown on the volcanic slopes of the Big Island of Hawaii.

"I just received a telephone call from Capt Grieg, reporting Cmdr Hoffman's arrest tonight for drunk driving and assaulting a Chief Petty Officer in the performance of his duties." Adm Hansen said, reading the Shore Patrols' Incident Report' off his computer.

"I warned Hoffman on three occasions to seek medical help for his drinking problem." Adm Porche said regretfully. "But it fell on deaf ears."

"The past year Hoffman became an alcoholic tyrant menacing the young Ensigns in his 'Intelligence Analysis' Section with a court-martial for any minor infraction, and took a sadistic pleasure in forcing them to resign from the Navy." Adm Porche said firmly. "I recommend Hoffman face charges before a court-martial or a forced retirement from the Navy!"

"Hoffman will be gone in 24 hours!" Adm Hansen said spotting a broad grin of satisfaction rise on the Marine's leathery Spanish American face.

"He was your Chief Intelligence Analyst. Did he compromise any of our intelligence work?"

"Hoffman tried to destroy a sensitive analysis report on a 'Chinese Submarine Incident,' but for the courage of a smart Ensign Puckett, we saved it in time." Sgt. Major Lopez said, smiling at Adm Porche.

Adm Hansen sat back and took another sip of coffee. *"I remember you guys coming in here two years ago with your 'Soviet Submarine Incident."*

"I'll never forget that young Ensign's 'Intelligence Analysis' detecting a Russian nuclear submarine that ran out of gas and sank in the middle of the Pacific Ocean."

"The President loved that line when we proposed locating and raising the lost Russian submarine."

"We had lots of fun for a year trying to keep the salvage operation a secret." Adm Hansen laughed refilling their coffee cups.

"I suppose you guys are here to give me a 'Top Secret' briefing on this new 'Chinese Submarine Incident."

"I've had a tough 12 hour day, and it's almost midnight. I'm booked solid all day tomorrow with my Fleet Admirals." Adm Hansen pleaded.

"Can't this wait a day or two?"

"No, Sir." Adm Porche said. "It can't wait!"

"There's a crisis in Korea!" The Night Duty Officer called out charging into Adm Hansen's office, followed by five senior Army, Navy, Air Force, and Marine CINCPAC staff officers.

Everyone gathered around Adm Hansen watching close up images of the infantry ground combat and the loud explosions of gunfire echoing around his office.

Sgt. Major Lopez's attention focused on 2nd / Lt. Smith hunkered down next to his Platoon Sgt Pickle in a muddy rice paddy while red North Korean AK 47 tracer rounds streaked overhead.

"What the hell's going on?" Adm Hansen demanded tense General Alexander Black, Commander 8th US Army Korea.

"One of my infantry platoons patrolling along the DMZ walked into a North Korean ambush an hour ago."

"There was a furious firefight while Lt. Smith and his platoon tried to break out of the ambush."

"Lt. Smith's Platoon is encircled by a battalion of 400 North Koreans!"

"He called in airstrikes to hammer the enemy so they can break out of the ambush."

"What the hell are you waiting for?" Adm Hansen roared angrily. "Strike fast and hard!"

"Send in flight of B 52's and A 10 WartHogs!"

"Hamburger those North Koreans!"

"The State Department wants us to sit tight while they try to negotiate Lt. Smith's platoon out of the North Korean ambush."

Gen Black said grimly.

"They are engaged in last-minute negotiations with the Pyongyang Regime over a nuclear arms verification agreement."

'The agreement has priority over any massive B 52 or A 10 airstrike."

Sgt. Major Lopez pushed his way through the Generals crowding around Adm Hansen's computer.

"I'd like to have a few words with Lt. Smith and his Plt. Sgt. Pickle to raise their morale while they wait to be overrun and killed by the North Koreans."

"I'm looking at you via our Centurion Satellite."

"You have a good defensive position from direct enemy fire. Dig in and conserve your ammo."

"The North Koreans are waiting for you to run out of ammo, then they'll go in for the kill."

"When you're outnumbered 1000 to 1, call in airstrikes and missiles."

"When you're outnumbered 10 to 1, call in your field artillery."

"If Gen George Armstrong Custer had brought his pack howitzers to the Little Bighorn, he could have turned the tide of battle and made a tactical withdrawal under covering fire of his howitzers."

"Do you think a field artillery solution will work for you?"

"Yes, Sgt. Major." Lt Smith replied. "We won't forget your tactical lesson."

"In 15 minutes, we'll begin pounding the enemy with 105 and 155 mm howitzers!"

"Cover your legs and butts with mud; hunker down in your flak jackets and helmets."

"We'll halt the barrage in 30 minutes to signal you to begin withdrawing on an azimuth of 180 degrees south."

"We'll support you with a rolling barrage while you lead your platoon out of the North Korean trap!"

"Radio in your fire request to your Division Artillery Fire Direction Center." Sgt. Major Lopez said firmly. "Do it now! Lt. Smith."

"Thanks for your help. Sgt. Major Lopez." Gen Black said giving a thumbs up to the Marine Top Sergeant. "Division Artillery is GO for your mission! I'll take any flak from the State Department until we get Lt. Smith's platoon safely back to our lines."

Sgt. Major Lopez took a sip of Adm Hansen's coffee and broke out in a broad grin. "When you're ready, Admiral, we have some unfinished business."

"This Korean Crisis gave me a shot of adrenaline." Adm Hansen said looking at his night duty staff officers. "I'm wide awake."

"Cancel all my appointments for tomorrow." He said leaving his Night Duty Officer in charge of his office. "I'm not to be disturbed until I call in, or we have another crisis."

"Let's take my jeep, Admiral." Sgt. Major Lopez said, driving towards the Pearl Harbor Navy Base.

"The last time we gave you a 'Top Secret' briefing, we were interrupted by a dozen staff officers rushing in and out of your office." The Chief of Naval Intelligence said grinning at his boss. "By morning everyone in Pearl Harbor was talking about the sunken Russian submarine."

"This time we've decided to conduct our 'Intelligence Briefing' in the most secure place in Pearl Harbor we're sure no one will interrupt us."

*****

28 ... Arizona Memorial

"This is the 'Arizona Memorial' launch!" The surprised CINCPAC Admiral said, boarding the launch with his Intelligence Officers.

"It was Sgt. Major Lopez's idea." Adm Porche said, looking at his Boss while they motored slowly across the moonlit waters of Pearl Harbor.

"I've never been out here at night!" Adm Hansen said, admiring the white marble Memorial bathed in the silvery moonlight.

Adm Hansen led the way up the white marble steps pausing a moment to join Admiral Porche and Sgt. Major Lopez, in a hand salute to the 'USS Arizona's' flag pole.

The CINCPAC Admiral removed his hat and knelt on one knee.

"Let's begin by paying homage to the 1177 officers and crew who rest in peace beneath us."

Adm Porche and Sgt. Major Lopez joined Adm Hansen in a moment of silent reflection to honor the crew and Officers and who made the ultimate sacrifice on Dec 7, 1941.

"I spend half my time as taking visiting VIPs, Heads of State, and Presidents on the Arizona Memorial recounting the Japanese attack on Pearl Harbor."

"This is my 1st private visit to this historical memorial."

"What a great place to discuss my problems with the officers and crew of the USS Arizona." Adm Hansen said. *"We're ready for you to begin your 'Intelligence Briefing.'*

Adm Porche set his Notebook PC on a marble bench and clicked down an electronic chart of the South Pacific Ocean.

"Three months ago, Sgt. Major Lopez gave one of my young intelligence analysts, Ensign Isaiah Puckett, a hard disk of ocean buoy and satellite tracking data on a Chinese submarine approaching the Marquesas Islands 1200 nautical miles southeast of Hawaii."

"Now watch this!" Adm Porche says tracking the icon with his electronic pointer.

"The Chinese submarine slows down, hits this volcanic island, and vanishes!"

"Ensign Puckett spots it, reports the mysterious Chinese Submarine Incident in his 'Daily Intelligligence Digest,' and turns it at the end of his watch."

"Cmdr Hoffman berates Ensign Puckett for being incompetent and turning in an unacceptable Intelligence Digest."

"He claims the satellite and sonar buoy data was faulty and feeds Puckett's 'Intelligence Digest' through a paper shredder!"

"Our curious Ensign saved a copy in his computer's hard disk for his reference, to wait and see if the Chinese submarine repeated the same course a few months later." Adm Porche said, pointing to Sgt. Major Lopez to continue the Intelligence Briefing.

"When Ensign Puckett turned the original hard disk back to me. He told me how Hoffman rejected his intelligence analysis of the Chinese Submarine Incident and put it through his shredder."

"Ensign Puckett was fighting mad! He charged Hoffman with being an incompetent alcoholic tyrant, and a disgrace to the Navy. He was ready to go back and punch Hoffman in the nose!"

"We both shared a visceral dislike for Hoffman." Sgt. Major Lopez said. "I calmed Puckett down and promised the next time the Chinese submarine disappeared under the Island. I would personally take his 'Chinese Submarine Incident' directly to Adm Porche."

"Ten days ago, Sgt Major Lopez brought me Puckett's 2nd Intelligence Report on the Chinese submarine." Adm Porche said, clicking down the latest satellite image on his computer monitor.

"Bingo!" He said solemnly watching the Chinese submarine surface then disappear under the ancient volcanic cone.

"Our satellite imagery of the volcanic cone indicates the five missiles are under the silo covers overgrown with guava bushes."

"This confirms Puckett's 2nd Intelligence Report describes a real event." Adm Porche said gritting his teeth. *"Let me read it to you!"*

Daily Intelligence Report
Prepared by Ensign Isaiah Puckett II
Data Analysis Section, Satellites and Ocean Buoys
Naval Intelligence Center, CINCPAC Pearl Harbor

This Chinese submarine is not a missile launch or attack submarine. Satellite Photos identify it as similar to ones used by the Imperial Japanese Navy during to support outposts on remote Pacific islands during WWII where it was too dangerous to send surface ships.

The Marquesas Islands 1200 miles southeast of Hawaii have many underwater lava domes and tubes used by the ancient Marquesans to bury their ancestors and warrior chiefs.

'A Chinese Missile Base inside an extinct volcanic cone on an uninhabited island in the Northern Marquesas ready to launch five nuclear tipped missiles at military and industrial centers in Hawaii, San Diego, Los Angeles, San Francisco, and Seattle, would strike a more deadly blow to the United States than the Japanese attack on Pearl Harbor that started WWII.'

Ensign Isaiah Puckett II

Sgt. Major Lopez watched Adm Hansen explode!

"That's pure speculation from a 24 year old Ensign going off half cocked with his imagination!"

Sgt. Major Lopez stepped in front of Adm Hansen and looked him coldly in the eyes.

"The 1st time you see your enemy preparing his attack."

"The 2nd time you confirm it."

"The 3rd time, Admiral. You're dead!"

"Do you know who you are sounding off too!" Adm Hansen roared again, pulling rank.

"Yes, Sir! The Commanding Officer of the USS Arizona!"

The Marine Top Sergeant snapped back coldly.

"In the early months of 1941, there were many intelligence reports from junior officers like Ensign Puckett warning Japanese Admirals were preparing surprise attacks on Pearl Harbor, Guam, Philippines, Singapore, and Australia."

"The Admirals and Generals in Hawaii and Washington rejected those young officer's warnings, failed to verify them, and incompetent officers like Cmdr Hoffman tried to destroy the careers of young junior officers like Ensign Puckett, who was honest and smart enough to recognize a potential enemy threat."

Adm Hansen reeled under the Marine Sergeant's frontal assault until calm objectivity replaced cold fury in his eyes.

"You're right, Sgt. Major. We have an obligation to those who paid the price for that bitter lesson!" Adm Hansen swore, pounding his fist on the white marble memorial. "It won't happen again under my watch!"

"Tomorrow I'll order a 'Centurion Satellite' placed in orbit over the Marquesas Islands, a dozen sonar buoys deployed by one of our submarines, and a Seal Team dropped on the island to recon Ensign Puckett's Chinese underground missile base."

"Have Ensign Puckett report to my office in the morning." Adm Hansen said cooling off. "I have an apology to make for the way Hoffman mistreated him."

"I want to thank him in person for getting his Intelligence Digest to us."

"We need young officers like Ensign Puckett with the' right stuff' to make a career in the Navy."

154

"I'm afraid it's too late. Ensign Puckett took his 30 day annual leave and flew to Tahiti 3 days ago." Sgt. Major Lopez said grinning at him.

"The next day, his roommate Ensign Green gave me this note."

> **To: Sgt. Major Pete Lopez**
> **"Gone fishing in the Marquesas Islands."**
> **Ensign Isaiah Puckett II**
> **"Who Dares! Wins!"**

"It's too dangerous! If the Chinese catch him, they'll kill him!" Adm Hansen roared jumping again to his feet.

"I'll order the local authorities in Tahiti to arrest Puckett and send him back to Hawaii!"

"Hear me through before having our young Ensign arrested." Sgt. Major Lopez said clicking down a brief summary on his computer screen.

"After I got his 'Gone Fishing Note.' I did a background profile on our Ensign Puckett."
"Let me read it to you."

Ensign Isaiah Puckett II USNR
Age: 24 years old. Home of Record: Nantucket Island, Cape Cod, Mass. B.Sc. Math, Physics. New England University. NROTC Reserve Commission.

"Members of Ensign Puckett's family have served our Nation with valor and courage going back to our War for Independence." Sgt. Major Lopez said proudly, taking the time to read the Roll Call of Puckett men who fought and died under the star-spangled banner.

1 st/ Lt. Jonah Puckett USMC.
The 1990 Gulf War. Bronze Star, Purple Heart.
Killed in Action.

Lt. Joshua Puckett, USNR.
Vietnam War, Navy Cross, Purple Heart.

Capt. Isaiah Pucket USNR.
War of 1812. Sank 2 Royal Navy Frigates and captured three others after fierce sea battles off the coast of England. Navy Cross, Purple Heart.

"In 1837 Capt Puckett used his 'Spoils of War' to build a whaling ship he sailed around Cape Horn to hunt the great whales for their baleen, excellent lubricating and crude lamp oil." Adm Porche said, continuing the Puckett family saga.

"He married a Vahine Tahiti, and they had five children before her tragic death in an 1849 smallpox epidemic."

"According to his roommate, Ensign Puckett took his 30-day annual leave to fly to Tahiti in search of his Tahitian family roots and Great Grandfather's legacy."

"What do you mean by 'Spoils of War'?" Adm Hansen asked warily.

"Was Capt Puckett a pirate?"

"His was an epoch of tall ships and iron men." Sgt. Major Lopez said grinning at the CINCPAC Admiral. "When iron-fisted Navy officers like Capt. Puckett led their Marines against our enemies with pistol and cutlass."

Adm Hansen, "Pirate cutlasses and spoils of war! He certainly has an interesting naval history."

"I'll have our military historian research Capt Puckett's history in our war of 1812 historical archives at Annapolis."

"Ensign Puckett had several months to plan his recon mission to the Marquesas." Sgt. Major Lopez said, continuing his briefing.

"First, he went to the Sonar Lab and asked to borrow a sensitive underwater microphone he needed to record fish sounds for his marine research project and his master's degree thesis."

"The Sonar Research Officers didn't buy his 'fish story' and threw him out!"

"Ensign Green told me he bought a similar underwater microphone and 10 meters of coaxial cable at a downtown Honolulu Music Shop, and sealed them with epoxy to make them watertight."

"They took the device down to one of our piers and tested it."

"Ensign Green told me they didn't record any fish sounds only noise from our warship engines and submarines."

"He borrowed a sensitive underwater imaging camera from the Navy Seal Unit."

"He told his friends he was going to the Marquesas Islands to do a marine research project for his master's degree"

"To create his image of a graduate student doing an important marine science research project, he showed them a collection of tropical fish books."

"Ensign Puckett is an intelligent young officer who works best on a mission critical assignment with a minimum of supervision."

Adm Porche said looking at Adm Hansen.
"He has to report back at the end of his 30 days leave."

"Let's give him a chance to accomplish his intelligence gathering mission."

"If you have no further questions?" Adm Porche said.

"This terminates our briefing on the Chinese Submarine Incident."

"It's been a long night." Adm Hansen yawned, watching Arizona's launch motor across the troubled waters of Pearl Harbor and tie up alongside the Arizona Memorial.

"Good morning! Gentlemen." A bright young Ensign in dress whites called out, bounding up the marble steps carrying a large triangular flag pouch under his arm.

"Did you have a pleasant visit on the Arizona Memorial last night?"

"The Memorial was beautiful and peaceful under the full moon." Adm Hansen smiled, watching the young officer unfurl 'Old Glory' from its pouch.

"A great place for a CINCPAC Commander to come and discuss his problems with Arizona's officers and crew."

"Raise Arizona's flag!" Adm Hansen called out to the young Ensign standing by the flagpole shining brightly in the 1st golden rays of a Hawaiian sunrise as 1177 officers and crew of the USS Arizona standing tall and proud in their dress white uniforms behind Admiral's Hansen, Porche, and Sgt. Major Lopez snapped to attention and paid homage with proud hand salutes to the Star Spangled Banner rising in the early morningbreeze, rippling the blue green waters of Pearl Harbor.

*****

29 ... Te Henua Enana

"Kaoha Nui I Te Henua Enana! / Welcome to the Land of Humans!" The melodious voice of the Air Manuroa hostess announced over the intercom. *"Please fasten your seat belts. We'll be landing in a few minutes."*

"The weather on Nuku Hiva is sunny and bright, temperature 30 C / 86 F with trade winds 15 to 30 knots. Our pilot and crew of Air Manuroa hope you enjoy your visit to the island of Nuku Hiva, and you'll fly again with us."

Hinano felt the vibration of the pilot reducing power on his twin turboprop engines, lower the landing wheels, and begin a steep descent touching down on the tarmac runway.

"Wake up, Isaiah." Hinano said, shaking him out of a sound sleep while the red and white aircraft rolled to a stop in front of the open-air terminal.

"Uncle Teiki's late!" She called out watching Marquesan families welcoming home their loved ones returning from Tahiti. Claim their luggage and cartons; they quickly loaded on four by four double cabin pickup trucks with oversized rough terrain tires to traverse the 2 1/2 hour drive over Nuku Hiva's rugged mountains to the Taiohae Village.

Isaiah offloaded their luggage, cartons, a plastic ice chest, and sat down next to Hinano in the open-air terminal to watch the departing Air Manuroa twin-engine airplane race down the runway, lift off, and climb into the white clouds floating above Nuku Hiva's jagged mountain peaks.

"I hope Uncle Teiki received your message on 'Radio Tahiti." Isaiah said, watching the last Marquesan family load their luggage and cartons on pack horses, gallop across the runway, and disappear into the dense brush of Nuku Hiva's high plateau.

"Here they come!" Hinano called out, pointing at two jeeps bursting out of the thick brush, race down the runway, and screech to a stop in front of the empty terminal.

Isaiah watched a deeply tanned barefoot Marquesan covered with tattoos wearing a pair of cotton shorts and a broad brimmed planter's hat, leap from his jeep beaming a broad cannibal grin, and rush over to greet Hinano and Isaiah.

Teiki's wife Tahia stepped off the second jeep wearing a bright red hibiscus crown on her pandanus hat, a yellow halter and pareo, carrying an armful of sandalwood leis to welcome her family from Tahiti.

"Kaoha Nui I Te Henua Enana!" Teiki and Tahia called out, welcoming Hinano and Isaiah with a light kiss on both cheeks and fragrant sandalwood leis around their necks.

"I'm ~ very ~ happy ~ to ~ meet ~ you ~ Uncle Teiki ~ and ~ Auntie ~ Tahia!" Isaiah said, waiting for Hinano to translate his greeting into their Marquesan language.

"We're ~ happy ~ to meet ~ you!" Teiki laughed with a deadpan American accent. "Welcome ~ to ~ Nuku Hiva."

"You speak excellent American English!" Isaiah said, shaking his Marquesan Uncle's calloused hand.

"Your visit will allow my family to practice and improve our American English."

"Our Puckett Valley is on the other side of that mountain." Teiki said pointing to a distant volcanic peak. "Help me lift your luggage, cartons, and ice chest onto my jeep's overhead pipe rack, and tie them down securely."

"I suggest you change your fancy Papeete clothes into something more suitable for the jungle." Tahia laughed at Hinano wiggling out of her silk dress into a pareo and Isaiah into his shorts and t-shirt.

"We're in for a wild, wet, muddy drive over a bush track, and we have to ford a mountain river before we arrive in the calm of our Puckett Valley."

"Isaiah will ride shotgun with Tahia in the lead jeep." Teiki called to his young Nephew from America. *"There's a chainsaw in back to clear any fallen trees. "*

"A shovel to dig the jeep out of any pig wallows and two pieces of PSP / Pierced Steel Planking to slide under the wheels if you get bogged down."

Tahia started her engine, shifted into four-wheel drive, hit the gas pedal with her barefoot, and sent the jeep roaring across the runway!

"Watch out you don't get slapped in the face by the spiny bushes!" She shouted, wrestling her jeep over two tire ruts winding through the bushes growing on Nuku Hiva's arid plateau.

Isaiah hung on for dear life until Tahia came to a halt at the edge of a mountainous slope falling into a narrow valley several hundred feet below.

"We'll hook the two jeeps in tandem to keep them from rolling over or sliding into a tree or boulder." Teiki shouted, shackling the two jeeps in tandem with a steel cable.

Slowly the jeeps crabbed and slid down the steep muddy mountainside into a deep ravine filled with triple canopy rainforest, 30 ft high bamboo, and giant ferns.

Tahia's jeep burst through a thicket of ferns, careened down a muddy riverbank, splash landing in a mountain river rushing down the valley!

"That was some splashdown!" Isaiah shouted, watching the ice-cold water rushing through the overheated jeep engine sending clouds of steam rising into the triple jungle canopy.

On the opposite river bank, two young Marquesans on horses galloped bareback into the river laughing at Isaiah and Hinano sitting waist-deep in the river rushing through the jeeps.

"These two wild ones are my daughter Tepua, 18 years old, and my son Teava, 22 years old." Tahia called out.

"Take this rope and lash it around the front bumper!" Teava shouted, tossing Isaiah a length of rope.

Isaiah jumped into the rapids, lashing the rope around the front bumper, leaping out of the way when Teava's horse began pulling his Mother's jeep up the opposite river bank.

Tepua's horse followed, pulling her Father's jeep out of the rapids onto the riverbank next to Tahia's sputtering but still running vehicle.

"Tomorrow morning we'll return with a team of horses and pull my drowned jeep down the valley into the workshop" Teiki laughed, jumping in the rear seat with Hinano.

"We graze a herd of beef cattle to provide us with steaks and roasts." Tahia smiled proudly, driving slowly past a herd of fat cattle. "A dozen dairy cows provide us with fresh milk and cheese."

"We have a herd of horses to ride and pull our work buggy."

"Our wild goats smoked in our ground oven or barbecued over a wood fire are tender and delicious."

"Our vanilla plantation," Teiki said, pointing proudly to bright green vanilla vines growing around their wood posts. "We have 1200 vanilla vines under culture near the head of our valley where it is shady and humid."

"With the price of grade 'A' vanilla beans nearly $80 a kilo in America."

"We plan to double our vanilla production and export directly to the USA."

"The archaeologists who studied this valley estimated more 100 Marquesan families were living here a 1000 years before the arrival of the first Spanish Conquistadors."

"Then came the Spanish in 1595 with their slave ships from Peru." Tahia said, recounting the dark history of her almost paradise valley to Isaiah and Hinano. "Over the next two centuries, Spanish slavers, English and French colonizers, and American whalers brought the white man's diseases."

"Tuberculosis, smallpox, typhoid, gonorrhea, and leprosy for which the natural immune systems of the pure race Marquesans had no resistance beginning mass extermination that lasted until the arrival of modern antibiotic drugs in the 1980s."

"Only the mixed-race Marquesans with the inherited resistance to the white man's diseases survived this mass extermination." Teiki said smiling at his wife. *"When I was a little boy, the last surviving families abandoned our valley, seeking a more modern life and jobs in Tahiti."*

"We're the last Marquesan family living in this valley."

"Let's stop for a snack." Tahia said, parking her jeep under a spreading mango tree growing on an ancient temple site.

"Follow me." Teiki said, handing Isaiah a bush knife to cut back the ground vines blocking the stone stairs leading past two moss-covered Tiki guarding the temple site.

"Our pristine islands and archaeological sites like this one offer opportunities as ecotourism destinations for my children and grandchildren to remain here and not abandon our valley for the outside world."

"I left my valley and islands when I was a young man to discover modern life in America." Teiki said with a concerned look on his face.

"After five years, I was fiu / I had enough and returned home to Nuku Hiva."

"Now, my son Teava and his sister Tepua want to visit America."

"Will they return someday or not?" Teiki asked the two stone-faced Tiki standing vigil over the ancient temple. "That is the question!"

"Let's go see if our Vahines are ready to go home." He said, leading Isaiah through the maze of stone ruins to Tahia and Hinano sitting under the mango tree devouring a bushel basket of ripe mangoes.

"Your Marquesan mangos are delicious." Hinano said, offering Isaiah and her Uncle Teiki a dozen juicy morsels.

"Hinano is always eating mangos." Teiki said laughing at his nephew. "She's a real Mango Vahine!"

"She loves mangoes." Isaiah laughed, holding up two golden ripe mangoes to make his point. "When I kiss her, she tastes mangoes."

"Do you have mangoes in America?" Tahia asked.

"I never saw mangoes in our Nantucket supermarkets."

"Hinano won't stay long in America." Tahia laughed.

"We'll have a June wedding on Nantucket Island and return to Tahiti before the next mango season."

"It's getting dark." Teiki said watching Tahia and Hinano load another basket of ripe mangoes in the back of the jeep. "Let's roll for home."

30 ... Teiki's Marquesan Home

The last violet and orange rays cast long shadows across the Puckett Valley when Tahia drove up to their plantation home and parked her jeep under a breadfruit tree next to two horses tethered to a lava rock watering trough.

"Welcome to our humble home!" Teiki said pouring a bucket of cold water over his head to wash off the sweat and grime with the help of a bar of coconut soap and a plastic scrub brush. *"Leave your muddy clothes in the laundry basin while you take a quick outside shower."*

Tahia rinsed off her naked husband with a bucket of cold water, threw him a towel, and a pareo he wrapped around his waist before charging up the stairs onto the veranda.

Tahia and Hinano stripped down and scrubbed each other with coconut soap and shampoo while Isaiah watched them laughing and enjoying their outdoor bath.

"Your towel and pareo are hanging on that tree branch." Hinano said, leaving him to finish his bath under the gaze of the Marquesan horses enjoying a handful of Hinano's mangoes.

"I'll go turn on the generator set!" Teava called out, rushing by in the darkness.

Isaiah wrapped his pareo around his waist and dashed up the stairs in time to see Teava throw the remote control circuit breaker on the wall, starting the diesel generator set in the workshop.

He stepped barefoot into the dining room, pausing a moment to admire the hand-woven bamboo lattice ceilings, lava rock walls, inlaid tou / rosewood floor tiles, and hand-crafted from giant golden bamboo.

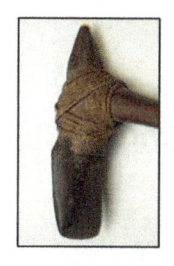

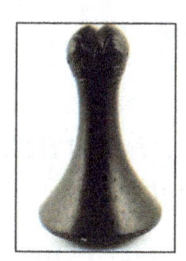

"Your home is a museum of Marquesan natural history and art." Hinano said, walking around the dining room studying the stone age artifacts; stone adzes, pearl shell fishing lures, rosewood umetes / bowels carefully arranged on shelves.

Teiki and his family sat around a rosewood dining table waiting for Hinano and Isaiah to finish the tour of their collection of Marquesan art and ethnology.

"Me Mai Kai Kai! / Come eat!" Tahia called out to Isaiah and Hinano.

"First, I have something special for you all!" Hinano said, handing out brightly wrapped gifts to Tahia, Tepua, and Teava.

"*Kou Ta'u! / Thank you!*" The Puckett Vahines said, opening their gifts of perfume and shampoo from Mama Puckett.

"*Kou Ta'u! Cousin Hinano.*" Teava said, kissing her on the cheek for her gift of the latest Tahitian and Marquesan CD's / Compact Disks.

"*Go load one in your boom box, Son.*" Teiki grinned at Teava. "*But not too loud.*"

"*A special gift for my Uncle Teiki and his family! A ice chest full of your favorite New Zealand ice cream packed in dry ice!*"

"*What a great treat!*" Uncle Teiki said, taking Hinano in a bear hug. "*We haven't tasted gourmet ice cream in almost a year.*"

"*Whoopee!*" Tahia, Tepua, and Teava shouted happily!

"*Dinner first!*" Teiki scolded his family. "*Save the ice cream for dessert!*"

Tahia bowed her head and began her prayer.

"*We ask your blessing on this food. We ask your benediction on our Cousin Hinano and her new Tane Isaiah. We wish them a long and happy life! Amen!*"

Isaiah's eyes widened in surprise at Tepua, lifting six U'a /Spiny Lobsters from the boiling water and serving them in rosewood umete / bowls to her family, waiting anxiously to crack open and devour her mouthwatering seafood delicacies.

Teava handed Isaiah a river rock to crack open the lobster shell. *"Try dipping the morsels into Tepua's whipped lime and butter sauce."*

"My Father and I are licensed lobstermen." Isaiah said, popping a piece of lobster tail in his mouth and making a loud slurping sound that informed everyone the Marquesan U'a was delicious.

"We dream about catching lobsters as big as yours!"

"Taste our Marquesan breadfruit poi cooked in our ground oven." Tepua smiled, serving Hinano and Isaiah a steaming portion wrapped in green banana leaves.

"Is it your Marquesan custom to eat with your fingers?"

"Yes, Isaiah." Tepua laughed. "Please don't make a mess on my nice clean floor."

"We have no secrets in our Puckett family." Hinano laughed, winking her eyebrows at Tepua and Tahia.

"Try our barbecue wild goat." Tahia said, carving off smoked ribs and serving them to Hinano and Isaiah.

"I've never eaten wild goat before. It's delicious!"

"I hope you all will someday come to visit our home." He said, smiling at Tepua and Teava.

"We would love to visit our Puckett family in America!" Tepua and Teava said, accepting Isaiah's invitation.

"After dinner, I have many color photos of my family, our Great Grandfather's home, our 36 ft commercial fishing boat 'Mary Puckett II,' and our 'Puckett Boat Shop' to show you."

*****

31 ... Ice Cream Frenzy

"If everyone's ready." Teiki said to his happy family, clearing the table and prepare Hinano's frozen dessert. *"Let's eat ice cream!"*

Teava quickly opened the ice chest and watched a white cloud of carbon dioxide float over the top as he reached inside and started pulling out his frozen treasure.

"Yum! Yum! Boysenberry!" Tahia said happily, grabbing her ice cream bucket. *"My favorite!"*

"Coconut is my favorite!" Tepua squealed with delight.

"Guava!" Teava shouted, opening his bucket.

"Where are your manners!" Teiki yelled at his family, digging into their favorite ice cream, making loud slurping sounds telling everyone the ice cream was delicious.

"Never mind!" Hinano exclaimed, eating her favorite mango ice cream. *"Enjoy yourselves!"*

Isaiah took out his video camera and recording Teiki's family having the time of their lives enjoying Hinano's ice cream treat from Tahiti.

When the ice cream feeding frenzy subsided, Tepua and Teava resealed the ice cream buckets and placed them in their home freezer.

"While Teava and Tepua are clearing the dining table, I'll show you to your bungalow." Teiki said, leading Hinano and Isaiah out the backdoor into a footpath leading into the moonlit coconut plantation.

"We have eight guest bungalows we rent to yachters sailing from the Galapagos through the Marquesas Islands to Tahiti."
"After three weeks at sea, the yachters and their crew like to spend a few days ashore to rest and recuperate after their long sea voyage."

"After rationing their freshwater and sleeping three weeks in a wet bunk, the yachters want a freshwater shower and a good night's sleep in a dry bed that doesn't rock and roll with every passing swell."

"They want a home-cooked meal with red meat, our garden picked vegetables, green salads, and all the tropical fruits we can supply them."

"We take them trekking in our valley, explore our Marquesan temples, photograph them with our stone Tiki, and enjoy an afternoon swimming under the waterfall at the head of our valley."
He said, leading Hinano and Isaiah into the Marquesan bungalow.

"We construct our guest bungalows using the same native materials used by our ancestors; ironwood post and beams, thatched roofs, and giant bamboo from our valley."

"Tepua decorated this double bed with two gardenia flowers on the pillow for you." He said, smiling at Hinano, enjoying the natural perfume filling the bungalow.

"Where's the toilet? Uncle Teiki."

"Go out the backdoor, down the stairs, and follow the footpath until you come to a hibiscus hedge."

"I put a bamboo gate at the entrance to keep our wild pigs from disturbing our guests while they make their toilet in the apo'o tupa / land crab holes."

"Take this pile of hibiscus leaves for your convenience." Uncle Teiki said, double winking his eyes at his Niece. "Dried hibiscus leaves, our traditional Polynesian toilet paper."

"Here is a mori pata / flashlight, and an umbrella in case of rain."

"Leave your luggage, and let's go back to the house." Uncle Teiki said, watching Isaiah unload two cartons with scientific instruments and a Navy gray military case.

"Tahia and Tepua will have an after-dinner snack and hot coffee to keep us awake while you recount your history of our common ancestors."

Isaiah pulled two brown envelopes from his flight bag and followed his Uncle Teiki and Hinano through the coconut plantation.

"During the day, solar panels on the roof charge a bank of heavy-duty batteries supplying us with DC power at night."

"After dark, we shut down the 220 / 110 volt AC generator set and switch over to our 24 volt DC batteries to power interior fluorescent lights, and my ham radio shack in a steel ocean freight container behind our home."

"Now watch when I shutdown the generator set in the workshop." Teiki said, pressing the 'Off' button on the AC remote control panel. "Notice how the ceiling fans slow down, and the entire house goes pitch dark."

"Now I'll push the 'On' button on the DC power control panel to open the circuit from the bank of batteries."

Isaiah watched the fluorescent tubes blink 'On' bathing the dining room in soft blue light.

"I have many modern conveniences for my family we didn't have when I was a little boy growing up in this remote valley 50 years ago." Teiki said, finishing his discourse on the impact of space-age technologies on his family's life on a remote island in the middle of the Great South Pacific Ocean.

"In a year or two, we'll be able to send or receive satellite television, telephone, and Internet; ending our isolation from the rest of the world."

"Let's go in and have a late-night snack while we listen to Isaiah recount the history of our famous ancestor." He said, joining his family around a rosewood coffee table while Tepua poured hot Marquesan coffee flavored with a snippet of vanilla bean and freshly squeezed coconut milk.

When everyone finished their after-dinner snack, Isaiah began his Great Grandfather's adventure and romance in Tahiti more than 150 years ago.

"In 1839 our Great Grandfather Capt Isaiah Puckett sailed his whaling ship 'Molly Puckett' into Papeete Harbor after nine months at sea hunting whales in the Roaring Forties of the Great Southern Ocean

"At a 4th of July tamara'a / banquet on the beach fronting the U.S. Consulate, he fell madly in love with a beautiful Vahine Tahiti."

"Her name was Hinareva Tauraatua, the youngest daughter of OeaTauraatua, High Chief of Paea Valley."

"How old was Hinareva when she married Capt Puckett?" Tepua asked.

"Mama Puckett said she was 16 years old." Hinano said, smiling at her Cousin.

"That's too young to get married!" Tepua exclaimed. "How old was Capt Puckett?"

"He was 48 years old."

"The old Billy Goat was old enough to be her grandfather!" Tepua shocked at Hinano's revelation.

"Wait a minute." Teiki called out. *"I was 33 years old when I married your 17-year-old Mother."*

"Am I an old Billy Goat?"

"Baaa! Baaa!" Tepua called out laughing at her Papa.

"Baaa! Baaa!" Tahia and Teava brayed at their old 'Billy Goat' tugging on his goatee.

The old Marquesan 'Billy Goat' looked up at the bronze wall clock striking midnight.

"We've all had a long day." He said, smiling at his tired but happy family.

"Why don't we continue Isaiah's family history in the morning." Isaiah said, looking at Hinano half asleep on the couch.

"We want to 'Thank You' for your wonderful Marquesan welcome and delicious dinner." Isaiah said pulling his tired Vahine to her bare feet.

"Goodnight Everybody!"

"Let's go for a moonlight stroll." Isaiah said, walking hand in hand with Hinano through the coconut plantation to their bungalow.

"This has to be the softest mattress I've had the pleasure to lie down upon." He yawned, stretching out his tired body.

"Tahia and Tepua made this mattress and pillows from kapok, silky fibers from a variety of tropical cotton trees they grow in their valley."

"Kapok was once widely used to make mattresses and pillows. Today most mattresses and pillows are made from synthetic foam rubber."

"Are you waiting for me to tuck you in?" Isaiah asked his Vahine, sitting nervously on the edge of the bed.

Hinano urgently, "I need to go to the toilet!" "I need to go now! I don't want to go outside alone!"

Isaiah lifted his bare butt off the kapok mattress, clicked 'On' his mori pata / flashlight, and followed his naked Vahine into the moonlit coconut plantation.

"Did you bring Uncle Teiki's hibiscus leaf toilet paper?" Isaiah whispered laughing at the thought of lowering his bare butt over a tupa crab hole. "I have more to lose than you!"

"Shuut! You'll wake up Uncle Teiki and his family." Hinano whispered following Isaiah along the footpath to another thatched bungalow, opened the bamboo gate, and looked for any wild tuskers inside a circular hedge of hibiscus flowers.

Isaiah opened the door and shined his mori pata around the inside of the bungalow.

180

"Do you see any unoccupied tupa crab holes?" She asked urgently.

Isaiah spotted a light switch, and read a sign bathed in the soft glow of orange lights hidden inside the bamboo walls.

"Welcome to the Puckett Throne Room!"

"Look at this deluxe porcelain toilet on top of this lava rock pyramid." Princess Hinano called out sprinting up the stepped pyramid, pirouetting like a ballet dancer, lowering her bare fanny on the rosewood throne, and gave Isaiah a happy sigh of relief!

"This is the most beautiful bathroom I've ever seen!" She called out from her throne.

"Uncle Teiki's 'Throne Room' is planted with orchids growing over a lava rock hanging garden!" Princess Hinano sighed happily!

"Don't move until I get my camera and take your 'Royal Portrait' on the throne!"

"Don't you dare! Isaiah Puckett." Princess Hinano laughed. *"Or I'll turn you into a tupa crab!"*

"Look around. The yachties left postcards, photos, and 'Thank You' notes from all over the world." He said, discovering a waterfall shower cascading off the rock wall into a sunken lava rock pool.

*****

32 ... A bright new day!

Isaiah watched Hinano mount up and gallop off trailing Tepua and Tahia into the early morning mist floating down the valley.

"Let's roll!" Teiki smiled, stepping lightly on the gas pedal, driving his jeep slowly along the bush track following the river rushing down the valley.

"What's that over there?" Isaiah asked, pointing at a crumbling lava rock and coral ruin on the river bank.

"A Saw Mill built by the English logging company in 1861."

"The sandalwood and rosewood logs were hauled out of the primal forest by horses, sawed into planks and beams, and shipped by three-masted sailing ships to Sydney, Auckland, San Francisco, and England.

"Everyone worked for the logging and trading company until the primal sandalwood and rosewood trees were depleted by 1889."

"Toma Puckett worked as a lumberjack until a Marquesan Warrior Chief killed him after he caught young Toma with his young wife."

182

"Did they eat him?" Isaiah asked.

"Toma was a young man in good health!" He said, making a loud slurping sound and giving everyone his best cannibal grin. "Long pig that runs on 2 feet! Prime meat not to be wasted!"

"We'll stop for a minute, check the generator set, and load up on ice chips to keep our fish cold." Teiki said, stopping his jeep in front of the plantation workshop built on a lava rock foundation by the English trading company.

"This is the ironwood keel of our new 36-foot boat. Teava and I should finish and launch the 'Tahia III' in about six months." Teiki smiled, running his calloused hands over the keel.

Isaiah, "My Father, like you, is a skilled boat builder and saltwater fisherman."

"Tonight, We'll make a ham radio telephone patch to your Dad on Nantucket Island, and I'll invite him to visit his Marquesan Puckett family."

"Teava is an excellent mechanic!" Teiki said, watching his son checking the 5-kilowatt diesel generator set humming smoothly on its rubber silent blocks.

*"Fuel level! .. OK!   Oil level! .. OK!
Batteries! .. OK"*

" Voltage 220! .. OK!   Water Level! .. OK!"

"Tepua and Teava jumped on my invitation to visit my Dad on Nantucket Island." Isaiah said, smiling at his Uncle and Cousin.

"He's hard-pressed to look after our Great Grand-father's three-story white house, rental cottages, and our fishing business during our summer tourist season."

"Teava could work part-time with my Dad in our 'Boat Shop' and go fishing with him our commercial fishing boat 'Mary Pucket II' on Nantucket Sound."

"Tepua could work part-time looking after the tourists who rent our beach cottages during our summer season."

"A 3 month 'paid working holiday' in America."

"Tepua and Teava will be safe with my Dad. An excellent way for them to discover America."

"You have a good idea. Tonight I'll discuss it with Tahia and see what she thinks about your invitation."

"Give us a hand loading the heavy sacks of ice chips in the jeep trailer." Teiki asked Isaiah shoveling ice chips in copra sacks.

Isaiah held on to his seat while Teiki drove slowly along the rocky quay to avoid breaking the springs on the overloaded jeep and ice trailer.

"Our quay was constructed from river rocks for the three-masted sailing ships from Sydney and San Francisco ...

... stopping over to load their precious cargo of sandalwood and rosewood timber." Teiki said recounting another facet of the 'Sandal and Rosewood Trade' in the Marquesas Islands.

"Every 6 months, an English ship dropped anchor to unload trading goods to pay the Marquesan loggers with carpenter tools, hammers, handsaws, wrought iron nails, pedal-powered sewing machines, cotton cloth, needles, thread; flour to make bread, rum, tea, and spices."

*"**Boat Day**' was always an essential event for the 100's of Marquesans and Englishmen who lived and worked in this valley between 1849 and 1889."*

"The ship's crew back loaded barrels of fresh water, salt pork, sundried fish, corned beef, firewood for the ships cooking stoves, fresh limes, and made any repairs to their sails and rigging."

"Today, many private yachts making the three week voyage across the South Pacific Ocean from Panama, and the Galapagos drop anchor in our bay for a few days before sailing to Tahiti."

"We enjoy their short visit, and they enjoy visiting a modern-day 'Robinson Crusoe' family!"

Isaiah leaped aboard the 'Tahia II' and started pouring the 50 kg ice chips into the fish hold while Teava checked the bamboo fishing poles, trolling hand lines, making sure the pearl shell and horse-hair lures were ready to go fishing.

"Let's go fishing!" Teiki shouted to Teava on the flying bridge.

Teava pushed the throttle forward, accelerating the 'Tahia II' across the bay; her bow throwing up plumes of salt spray as she surfed the dark blue oceanic swells rising from the depths of the South Pacific Ocean.

Isaiah sat on the flying bridge next to his Uncle Teiki and Teava watching the fiord like valley and oval bay merge into the cloud covered mountains thrust up from the Pacific Ocean to form a volcanic island the ancient Marquesans named Nuku Hiva.

Isaiah sat on the flying bridge next to his Uncle Teiki and Teava watching the fiord like valley and oval bay merge into the cloud-covered mountains thrust up from the Pacific Ocean to form a volcanic island the ancient Marquesans named Nuku Hiva.

"Give your horse his head!" Tahia shouted at Hinano, galloping up the narrow bush track winding through the coconut plantation.

"How far up your valley is the coffee plantation?" Hinano called out to Tepua racing ahead on her black stallion.

"About one and a half kilometers." Tepua shouted back.

"Yahoo!" Tahia shouted, jumping over a family of wild pigs wallowing in the bush track, scattering them squealing and grunting into the jungle.

The three Vahines reined in and dismounted in the cool shade of a mango tree on the riverbank.

"Let your horse run free." Tepua said, stuffing a mango in her stallion's mouth. *"They'll graze in the meadow, snack on ripe mangos, and play in the river until we're ready to go home."*

"We should be able to fill three copra sacks with ripe beans!" Tepua said, leading Tahia and Hinano up the mountainside covered coffee trees sagging under the weight of ripe red beans.

"Tell us about your new Tane." Tahia asked Hinano stripping handfuls of ripe coffee beans into her bucket.

"He's an intelligent and gentle young man."

"Does your Tane have many tattoos on his muscles?"

"No, Tepua. It's not their custom."

"Most popa'a / white men smell like Billy Goats." Tepua laughed.

"I make him shower 2 or 3 times a day to keep him clean and smell good." Hinano said, stripping a handful of ripe coffee beans into her bucket.

"What is he like when you have sex?" Tepua giggled, throwing a ripe coffee bean at Hinano.

Tahia, "Ieee! Tepua. That's none of your business." Hinano, "Can you keep a secret?"

"Oh! Yes!" Tepua and Tahia giggled. "Your secret will never leave this valley!"

"Get ready to go fishing!" Teiki shouted, pointing at 100's of black frigate birds, white fairy terns, brown boobies, and red-tailed tropic birds diving into a school of sardines ...

... in a frenzied attempt to escape the skipjack, yellowfin tuna, mahi-mahi, dolphins, marlin, and oceanic sharks that were feeding on them.

Teava accelerated the 'Tahia II' to 12 knots surfing over the long oceanic swells on a direct course with the feeding frenzy.

"We use the same bamboo pole, and pearl shell lures our ancestors used when they went fishing in their outrigger sailing canoes a 1000 years ago!" Teiki shouted handing Isaiah a 4 meter / 12 ft. bamboo fishing pole with a heavy nylon line and pearl shell lure.

"Cast your lure over the stern when Teava turns into the seething mass of sardines and diving seabirds!"

"When you get a strike, haul the fish over the stern rail as hard and fast as you can!"

Isaiah hooked the 1st yellowfin tuna! A 20-kilo 'gorilla', he wrestled over the boiling wake of the fast-moving boat.

Teiki set the gaff behind the gills and struggled to haul the fighting fish over the stern rail.

Isaiah leaped in next to his Uncle, grabbed the gaff, gave a mighty pull, threw the 'gorilla' tuna, and his Uncle sprawling on deck!

"You, OK? Uncle Teiki." He asked, pulling him back on his feet with his free hand.

Isaiah and Teiki grabbed their bamboo fishing poles and caught four more yellowfin tuna before the school of sardines plunged to the safety of the ocean depths.

"We caught a dozen skipjack tuna and five yellowfin tuna in less than 30 minutes!" Isaiah shouted joyfully.

"Let's troll for mahi-mahi!" Teiki called down to Teava and Isaiah gutting the gorilla tuna, pack them in ice chips, and lower them into the fish hold.

"We use a pearl shell lure with a horsehair tail that looks like our marara / flying fish to hungry mahi-mahi." Teava said, pulling two coils of nylon hand line and cowhide gloves from the tackle box.

Teava and Isaiah pulled on leather gloves, played out two mahi-mahi lures, and waited for the 1st hit.

Isaiah struck the gaff into the fighting fish and tossed it flopping on deck.

"This is the 1st time I've seen live mahi-mahi." "Look at the rainbow of colors. What a beautiful fish!"

"Wait until you taste it," Teava called to his cousin. "Charcoal broiled or grilled in a lime and butter sauce."

Isaiah got the 2nd strike! Another 15-kilo mahi-mahi!

"Isaiah invited them to visit his father, Joshua." Hinano said smiling reassuringly at her troubled Auntie.

"His Father's been living alone in their Great Grandfather's white house since Isaiah went into the US Navy."

"Isaiah says Tepua and Teava could spend a three-month working holiday with their Uncle Joshua."

"Tepua could look after the tourists who rent their summer cottages."

"Teiki and I are very proud of our daughter."
Tahia whispered admiring Tepua's natural beauty
while feeding a dozen ripe mangoes to her horses.

*"She wants to go with her brother to America.
We are afraid of what will happen to them."*

*"When she promenades down Nantucket's ocean
beach with her Marquesan papaya on display in a
bikini, she will drive those young American men
wild with joy!"*

"That's what worries me!" Tahia said, splashing
cold water on Hinano and Tepua.

The sun was high and hot when Teiki throttled
the 'Tahia II' slowly against the quay while Isaiah
secured the bowlines to the mooring buoy, and
Teava tied the stern lines to the cast iron bollards.

*"Isaiah and I will filet a tuna for lunch and pack
the rest in our freezer."* Teava said, helping Isaiah
haul the ice-cold fish out of the hold and place them
under canvas cover in the jeep's trailer.

*"Bring a filet of yellowfin tuna into the kitchen
for lunch while I clean the boat, refuel, and get her
ready for our next fishing trip!"*
Teiki shouted after Teava and Isaiah.

"I'll bet Tahia and Tepua are swimming and playing in the river, exchanging gossip and family news with Hinano."

"Let's have some cold fruit and juice to quench our thirst while we wait for our Vahines." Teiki said, taking a plate of frozen grapefruit slices and a pitcher of pineapple juice from the refrigerator and set them on the kitchen table.

"Try our Marquesan grapefruit." Teiki said, pushing the plate to Isaiah. "We have a citrus grove of grapefruit, oranges, and limes for our use and the surplus we sell to passing yachts."

"Your grapefruit is sweet as honey." Isaiah said, helping himself to the midday fruit snack.
"That was some joke you played on us last night."

"Hinano and I went out with the mori pata, and hibiscus leaves looking for 'unoccupied' tupa / crab holes to make our toilet as you told us to do."
"What a surprise when we walked into your 'Throne Room."

"Hinano was the happiest Vahine in the Marquesas when she discovered your American porcelain toilet perched atop the lava rock pyramid."

"When I was a boy, we had to make our toilet over a tupa hole and use dried hibiscus leaves." Teiki said laughing at the thought. "Many times, I had to leap out of the way of an angry tupa crab ready to cut off my family jewels with his pincers."

"During my five years in America, I discovered your porcelain toilets with comfortable seats."

"Before I returned home, I bought a deluxe model in a Hollywood plumbing store and shipped it back by freighter to Nuku Hiva."

"I mounted it on the lava rock pyramid, added the sunken tub, and the waterfall shower. Tahia and Tepua planted the tropical flower garden."

"It was the passing yachters who named it the ...

The Puckett Throne Room."

"You never told us you visited Hollywood!" Teava said, surprised at his Father's revelation. "I want to hear your 5 year adventure in America."

"You and Tepua were too young." Teiki laughed.

"I too, would like to hear your adventures in America." Isaiah said, looking at his Uncle Teiki. "How about tonight? Papa, right after dinner!"

Teiki laughed at his Son and Nephew's curiosity.

"OK! You guys. Right after dinner."

*****

33 ... A New Polynesian Custom

"Here they come!" Teava shouted looking out the window at Tahia leading her coffee caravan through the coconut plantation. *"Let's go give them a hand with the heavy sacks of coffee beans."*

Teiki lifted a sack of coffee beans off Tahia's mount and carried it on the veranda. *"We have a filet of yellowfin tuna for lunch."*

Hinano glared at Isaiah, admiring Tepua's bare breasts bouncing up the stairs into the house. *"You can carry my sack when you are ready! Isaiah Puckett."*

"I'm sorry, this is another custom my eyes will have to get used too." Isaiah apologized to his Vahine.

"You Tanes caught and cleaned the fish." Tahia winked at Hinano and Tepua to give a helping hand. *"We'll prepare lunch while you set the table."*

"Can I look over your shoulder while you show me how to make marinated fish?" Isaiah asked Tepua, cinching her pareo over her bare breasts.

 "I'm sure my Dad would like to try your marinated fish recipe made with our bluefin tuna and flounder."

"First, we chop a kilo of yellowfin tuna into morsels we place in a large salad bowl." Tahia said, smacking her lips at the sight of the fresh filet of yellowfin tuna on her cutting board.

"Blend in the freshly squeezed juice of 1 or 2 limes, a pinch of black pepper, and a tablespoon of salt to marinate the raw fish."

"Cut up and blend in tomatoes, lettuce, onions, and cucumbers, when the raw fish turns white and firm to taste."

"How long does it take to marinate?" Isaiah asked.

"You may want to marinate four hours in your refrigerator." Tahia smiled, popping a tasty morsel of raw fish in her mouth. "We can't wait more than five minutes!"

"You discovered we rise at 4 am." Uncle Teiki said, watching Isaiah devouring his Auntie's delicious marinated fish. "Hinano, Tahia, and Tepua left on horseback at dawn to spend the morning harvesting coffee at the head of our valley."

"We left the quay at sunrise and spent the morning fishing aboard the 'Tahia II."

"Our Island of Nuku Hiva is 7 degrees below the equator, so we try to do our hard work during the coolest part of the day in the early morning and finish before high noon."

"It's our custom to take a siesta after lunch during the hottest part of the day, noon to 3 pm."

"After our siesta, we'll work on our new fishing boat in the cool shade of the workshop."

"Tahia, Tepua, and Hinano will do some light housekeeping and laundry in the cool shade of our home." Teiki said, smiling at Isaiah and Hinano.

"I hope you are enjoying your working holiday with your Marquesan 'Robinson Crusoe' family."

"We're having a great adventure with your family in your 'Almost Paradise' valley." Hinano said, smiling at her Uncle Teiki and Auntie Tahia.

"Let's go take a cool shower under the waterfall before we take our siesta." Hinano said, walking hand in hand with Isaiah through the coconut plantation.

"I want to soak in the sunken lava rock tub in Uncle Teiki's 'Throne Room.'"

"After we're married and return to Tahiti."
"I'll build a tropical bathroom onto your home with a waterfall and sunken tub lined with polished lava rocks."

"We'll call it **'Hinano's Throne Room.'**"

"I'll make it into a beautiful tropical garden filled with ferns, red torch ginger, and climbing orchids." She said, giving Isaiah her kiss of approval.

"What happened to you?" Isaiah asked, watching her slip off her torn panties.

"Tepua's pet Billy Goat spotted us eating mangoes and trotted over for a handout." She said watching Isaiah examine her holed panties.

"Old Billy began eating my panties right off me."

"I wonder why did he did that?"

Isaiah sniffed the torn panties and started laughing. "We both have a taste for sweet juicy mangos."

"Ieeooh! Isaiah." She laughed. "You're a real savage!"

"Baaa! Baaa!" Her horny Billy Goat brayed, pulling his Vahine under the waterfall.

"You have beautiful long hair." He said, reaching for a shampoo bottle left behind by the passing yachties.

"Let me help you wash it." Isaiah laughed, lathering her hair and drawing soapy finger paintings on her sun bronzed butt.

"Are you enjoying yourself?" She giggled.

"I'm having the time of my life with you." He said, rinsing her under the waterfall holding her hand while she stepped down into the lava rock pool and floated into his warm embrace. "Every day I spend with you is a new romance and adventure."

"Did you have a good time in the valley this morning with Tahia and Tepua harvesting coffee beans?" Isaiah asked his Tahitian mermaid floating in his arms.

"It was my first time riding bareback. Marquesan horses respond easily to touch, and body commands. It was great fun!"

"When we go home to Nantucket Island."

"We'll take our beach buggy and a picnic basket." He reminisced, glancing at his Vahine dreaming happily in his arms.

"We'll spend our warm August nights camping in some remote cove where we can watch the shooting stars streak across the night sky."

Isaiah, "You haven't heard a word I said to you!"

"I heard everything you said." Hinano whispered softly.

"Every time you start talking about your home and family on Nantucket Island, her dream comes back to me."

"Hinareva wants to come with us to Nantucket Island. She wants to be reunited with her Tane!"

"Do you think your Great Grandfather misses his beloved wife?"

"I'm sure he loves and misses her very much," Isaiah said, sitting straight up under the waterfall.

"It was you who came here to find your family and heritage." She said, giving him a serious look. "When you wept on her grave, your tears of joy touched her heart and awakened her soul and spirit."

"Will your Great Grandfather be happy if we don't take Hinareva back with us?" Hinano asked fearing his wrath and anger.

"The Old Pirate's ghost will be so angry he will chase after us at night with his cutlass!"

"What do you want me to do?" Isaiah asked anxiously. "Dig up her remains, fly them back in a casket with her tombstone, and bury her next to her husband!"

"No! Isaiah." Hinano said looking at her troubled Tane. "We'll bring her tu'pau'pau/ ghost with us."

Isaiah gave up, trying to rationalize the irrational and accepted Hinano's decision. "You use your magic to put Hinareva's spirit in a bottle of your monoi."

"We'll carry her back to Nantucket Island on the jet, and you can let her ghost out of the monoi bottle on my Great Grandfather's grave. Will that make you and Hinareva happy?"

"That's a wonderful idea!" Hinano sighed happily.

"I'll conduct our ancient Tahitian chants on your family marae to reunite Capt Puckett and his beloved Hinareva."

"I think they'll be more than impressed." He laughed, taking his Tahitian mermaid in a loving embrace.

"I'll conduct our ancient Tahitian chants on your family marae to reunite Capt Puckett and his beloved Hinareva."

"I think they'll be more than impressed."
He laughed, taking his Tahitian mermaid in a loving embrace.

"We'll celebrate Hinareva's reunification with Capt Puckett, with a Tahitian tamaraa / feast on the beach fronting our home."

"I didn't think you believed in ghosts?"

"I didn't believe in ghosts, magic, and witches," Isaiah said, kissing his tahua / Tahitian witch. "Until I met and fell in love with you!"

*****

34 ... Teiki's Ham Radio Shack

"Let's go into my ham radio shack and see if we can make a phone patch to your Father on Nantucket Island." Teiki said, looking at Isaiah.

"Go with him!" Tahia scowled. *"He spends more time talking to his friends on the ham radio than he does with me."*

"Close the door behind you, so we don't get blown away by the noise and static."

"Don't forget your promise." Teava reminded his Father. *"Tonight, we want to hear your adventures in America."*

"Your Papa has many wild tales to tell about the Hollywood actresses who admired his muscles and tattoos before he married me."
Tahia said, teasing her old Billy Goat.

"Fiu! / That's enough! Leave me in peace!"
He grumbled, leading Isaiah out the back door to a 20-ton steel ocean freight container on concrete blocks next to a 3-meter satellite antenna pointing north to the equator.

"Welcome to my ham radio shack." Teiki grunted, pushing open the heavy steel door and pointing to the ham radio ...

... antenna tuner, and satellite decoder on the end table of his ham radio shack.

"The container is air-conditioned and sealed to keep bugs and humidity from destroying my electronics."

"Today, I can send ham radio messages to an amateur radio satellite that passes overhead and relays them all over the world." Teiki said slipping on his earphones and changing frequencies to sort the voice traffic from the cacophony of space noise and static filling the ham radio shack like a runaway boom blaster. *"It's 8 pm, time to check in with my contact in America."*

Isaiah tried to follow his Uncle's transmissions. Still, after a few minutes, his inability to decipher the jargon and coded language of the radio amateurs through the dissonance of background noise and static quickly turned off his interest.

He looked for a diversion in the dusty paper back books and magazines left behind by the visiting yachties until a faded green beret next to a tattered photo album caught his attention.

Sgt Teiki Puckett Vietnam War Photo Album

"These photos in Uncle Teiki's album are similar to those in my Father's Vietnam War photo album." Isaiah mused, slowly turning the pages.

Photos of US Army Private Teiki Puckett during his Basic Training at Ft. Ord, California; Parachute and Ranger Courses at Ft. Benning, Georgia; Special Forces Course at Ft. Bragg, North Carolina; and the Jungle Warfare Course in Panama.

Photos of Staff Sergeant Teiki Puckett leading his Montagnards along the Ho Chi Minh trail matched his Dad's experiences as a Navy Seal ferreting out the Viet Cong in the U Minh forest.

On the last page, he read the citation awarding Sgt. Teiki Puckett the Silver Star and Purple Heart medals.

*****

35 ... Adventures of a young Marquesan

"Teava!" Teiki said looking at his handsome tattooed son. *"You're now a grown-up 22 year old Tane api."*

"Tepua!" He smiled proudly at his beautiful daughter. *"You're now a grown-up 18 year old Vahine api."*

"You both want to visit America as I did 30 years ago. Go visit Isaiah and your Uncle Joshua on Nantucket Island."

"Learn the lessons from my misadventures."

"But never forget your home and valley in Henua Enana / the Land of Humans." He said beginning his adventures as a young man setting out to discover the world.

"In the 1960s, fewer than 1000 Marquesans were living in isolated villages scattered over an island archipelago the size of the Hawaiian Islands."

"We a few primary schools but no public high schools. When I was 14 years old, my parents sent me to a boarding lycee / high school in Papeete, Tahiti."

"On weekends and holidays, I stayed with Mama's family in Paea. She is the 'living memory' of our family history and genealogy."

"I could sit for hours on the veranda listening to her recount the love story of Capt Puckett, his beloved Hinareva and his adventures hunting whales in the Great Southern Ocean."

"The mystery of what happened to Capt Puckett and his two eldest children Sarah and Joshua after their return to America following the tragic death of Hinareva in the 1849 smallpox epidemic intrigued every generation of our family."

"When I graduated from high school, I decided to go to America, find my American Puckett family, and discover the heritage left behind by our Great Grandfather."

"I had the same mission as you." Teiki said, smiling at Isaiah. "To search for and reunite our Puckett family."

"My Marquesan Uncle Timi came to visit Mama's family whenever his ship the **'O Te Manu'** / 'Follow the seabirds' came into the Port of Papeete to discharge cargo from New Zealand or Los Angeles.

"Uncle Timi was one of the last master tattoo artists using the ancient handmade tools to apply tattoo body art on the skin with traditional dyes made from our plants and trees. Most of my tattoos are his artwork." He said, showing Isaiah the tattoos on his muscled chest, arms, and legs.

36 ... Hollywood

"In 1970, I tossed my seaman's bag over my shoulder, bid 'Farewell' to Uncle Timiona, walked down the gangway onto the Port of Los Angeles." Teiki said, recalling his adventures as a young man in America. "And began my search for my American Puckett family."

"Didn't Mama tell you the 'Home Port' for Capt Puckett's Whaling Ship was Nantucket Island in the Atlantic Ocean?" Isaiah asked. "Not the Port of Los Angeles on the Pacific Ocean."

"That detail got lost somewhere in time." Teiki laughed at his youthful innocence. "I began my quest in the waterfront seaman's bars."

"Was your Great Grandfather rich or poor?" The Barmaid asked, serving me a cold beer.

"He owned a whaling ship."

"Then he must have been rich." She said. "All the rich people live in Beverly Hills and Hollywood."

"Try looking for his family name in the telephone book at the end of the bar.

"I copied down several Puckett telephone numbers, from the Beverly Hills telephone book, and began dialing."

"Good morning!" The Maid would answer. *"This is the Puckett Residence. Can I help you?"*

"My name is Teiki Puckett. I just arrived by ship from Tahiti. I've come to visit my Puckett family in America."

"I think their curiosity got them interested in sending a chauffeur to pick me up at the Port."

"My new Puckett family invited me to spend a few days as their house guest in their Beverly Hills mansion."

"They gave me their best guest room with maid service, and every morning I swam in their heated heart-shaped swimming pool."

"I entertained them with tales of our Puckett family in Tahiti and growing up in the remote Marquesas. They were fascinated by my history of Capt Puckett and Hinareva." Teiki said, smiling at Tepua and Teava. *"I discovered a great way to visit America."*

"Your Papa has been telling the same pack of lies to his family for 25 years!" Tahia called out, pointing her finger at her Tane. *"When his Army buddies came to visit on their yachts, your Papa sent his wife and children to bed right after dinner."*

"The next morning, while you and your Army buddies were sleeping off your drunken fete, their wives came ashore in their dinghy for coffee and tea." Tahia said grinning at her Tane.

"They were very helpful translating your Papa's colorful expressions and profanity."

"I'm sure they were very interested in helping you," Teiki said wryly. "I tried to teach you only polite correct American English."

"I wanted to protect you and our children from my misadventures as a young man without any guidance or worldly experience."

"Now that your children have grown up." Tahia laughed at her Tane. "Tonight they're going to listen to their Papa tell us the true stories of his misadventures in America."

"Tepua! Go fill two pitchers of pineapple juice." She said, placing a hand-carved umete / bowl in the center of the coffee table.

"Teava! Bring two bottles of your Papa's 'Old Pirate Rhum,' shave ice, and a vanilla bean!"

Tahia blended the rhum, pineapple juice, and vanilla, stirring it to taste with a bamboo paddle.

"*How do you like my rhum punch?*" She asked, offering her Tane a glass of his favorite firewater.

"*Delicious!*" Teiki said smacking his lips. "*It has a kick like a mule.*"

"*A toast to our newly grown-up Daughter and Son.*" Tahia said smiling at Tepua and Teava tasting their 1st rhum punch. "*Manuia! / Cheers!*"
"*May your visit to Uncle Joshua in America be a rewarding and prosperous experience.*"

"*Manuia!*" Isaiah and Hinano offered to raise their glasses in honor of their Auntie's toast.

"*Enjoy yourself.*" Tahia said draining her first glass of rhum punch and refilling again from the umete bowel. "*But learn to control yourself and know when to stop before you get roaring drunk like your Papa.*"

"*I'll tell the 1st story as I learned it from my Billy Goat's mouth.*" She said, pointing her finger at her Tane quietly, sipping his rhum punch on the couch next to his children listening to her every word.

"*Your Father found a great way to discover America.*" Tahia said taking another long drink of fiery rum punch. "*He went from one Puckett family to the next regaling them with tall tales of Tahiti and the Marquesas.*"

"In Hollywood, our young Marquesan 'Tarzan' met his movie actress cousin Pamela Puckett who lived in a pink marble mansion with a heart shaped swimming pool in her landscaped garden.

Pamela was in her seventies, divorced five rich husbands, and remodeled several times by the best plastic surgeons in Hollywood."

"A female tiger shark who devoured every man she met!" Tahia said finishing off her 2nd glass of fiery rhum punch.

"A real live maneater!"

"Pamela transformed her mansion's landscaped gardens into an outdoor art gallery with marble statues of ancient Roman and Greek demigods; Nike, Poseidon, Jupiter, Hercules, and 'Tarzan."

"Our 'Marquesan Tarzan' was her living masterpiece of tattoo body art. To celebrate, she organized a private cocktail party and art show for her movie actress friends on her poolside patio."
Tahia called our pointing her finger at her Tane.

"Can you imagine the carnal pleasure those movie actresses had ogling and caressing the tattoos on Teiki Puckett's chest muscles, arms, and legs, while he tried to stand motionless, stark naked, on the cold marble pedestal!"

"Enough!" Teiki protested. *"You're exaggerating again."*

"Like hell, I am!" Tahia retorted. "You were too drunk to remember."

"Do you want me to quote what you said those lusting movie actresses did to you while you stood stark naked on the pedestal!"

Teiki looked around at everyone staring at him while he downed another glass of rum punch and stoically waited for his wife to finish her verbal flagellation for his youthful excesses.

"Teiki Puckett's promising career as a Hollywood sex symbol was cut off at the short hairs by another jealous husband who had him arrested, jailed, and charged with being an illegal alien working as a male model and tattoo artist without a business license."

"Papa! You never told us you went to jail!" Tepua and Teava cried out.

"Your Father has lots of secrets he's hidden from us." Tahia said. "Now it's his turn to tell us what happened next."

Teiki looked around at his shocked family, waiting for him to begin his next misadventure in America.

"I was taken before a Los Angeles Federal Immigration Court, where I explained to the Judge my reason for coming to America was to find my American family."

"He was very interested in my history of Capt Puckett and Hinareva." Teiki looked around at his shocked family, waiting for him to begin his next misadventure in America.

"I was taken before a Los Angeles Federal Immigration Court, where I explained to the Judge my reason for coming to America was to find my American family."

"He was very interested in my history of Capt Puckett and Hinareva."

"I have two options." The Judge explained.

"I can order you deported immediately on the next cargo ship for Tahiti, or I can give you a temporary resident permit if you enlist for two years in the US Army."

"When you receive your Honorable Discharge, you can become a naturalized US Citizen and continue your quest for your family, live, and work in the United States as long as you want."

"The next morning, I was released in the custody of an Army Recruiter, signed the two year enlistment papers, and by noon I was on a bus headed for a nine-week Basic Infantry Training Course."

"US Army Private Teiki Puckett graduated from boot camp at the head of his training battalion." Teiki said proudly.

"At the end of my Advanced Infantry Training Course, I was interviewed by a green beret Colonel recruiting soldiers with high scores to join his Special Forces Group at Ft. Bragg."

"I liked the 'gung ho' spirit of the soldiers in my Special Forces Group. We had great fun at the Airborne Parachute and Ranger Courses at Ft. Benning."

"I showed the Jungle Warfare Officers in Panama how to marinate rattlesnake meat with a pinch of salt and lime juice." Teiki said, laughing at the grimaces on his family's faces.

Teiki noticed Tepua, Teava, and Hinano getting bored and sleepy listening to his war story while Tahia slipped into a drunken stupor.

Only Isaiah listened, analyzing his every word.

*****

214

37 ...The Vietnam War

"A 2 star General flew down from Washington to present our green berets and the colors of our new Special Forces Group while we marched proudly in review to the rousing music of the Ft. Bragg Army Band."

"A few days later, we loaded our new Special Forces Group aboard a fleet of US Air Force C 141 Starlifters and flew off into the night sky."

"After a 24 hour flight across the Pacific Ocean, we touched down at Danang, South Vietnam. My 'A' Team boarded a flight of HUID Helicopters and flew into the highlands near the Laotian border."

"While Army helicopters suppressed incoming enemy fire, we landed on a mountaintop redoubt held by a Special Forces' A' Team and a Company of Laotian Montagnards."

"PFC Teiki Puckett landed right in the middle of the Vietnam War!"

"Our mission was to conduct LRRP / Long Range Recon Patrols ferreting out NVA / North Vietnamese Army units and supplies moving down the Ho Chi Minh trail and target them for Air Force B 52 Bomber strikes."

Teiki noticed Isaiah gave him a look that struck fear in his heart. "Is there something bothering you?"

The cold look receded, and Isaiah once again broke out in a broad smile. "Its nothing, Uncle Teiki. Please continue."

"I'm very interested in hearing your war story."

"I spent the next 18 months searching out NVA / North Vietnamese units, and targeting them for B 52 strikes." He said focusing his attention on his Nephew. "Then, our luck ran out."

"Early one morning, we walked into a North Vietnamese ambush while we were returning to our mountaintop redoubt."

"During the firefight, I got whacked in the head by mortar shrapnel that put me in a coma for several days. The NVA left me for dead on the battlefield."

"I woke up with a splitting headache, dressed my wounds, and looked around to see if anyone else was alive. I was the sole survivor!"

"I snared and ate red jungle fowl, and rested for several days to regain my strength before returning to my Special Forces redoubt."

"I crawled through the minefield at night to avoid any enemy waiting to finish their work at the barbed wire perimeter."

"I gave the dog tags from our dead to my 'A' Team Leader and a report on my recon mission. I had been reported dead or missing in action."

"Army Special Forces Sergeant Teiki Puckett was flown to Oakland Army Hospital in California. While my wounds healed, my only thought was to return to my home and valley in Te Henua Enana / The Land of Humans."

"I mustered out at Oakland Army Terminal three months later; returned to Los Angeles to pick up my Naturalization Papers and US Passport from the Federal Judge who four years before volunteered me for the Vietnam War."

"My movie actress Cousin Pamela invited me to spend a couple of weeks R & R / Rest and Recueration in her Hollywood mansion while I waited for Uncle Timi and the 'O Te Manu' to take me home to Tahiti." Teiki said, looking at Isaiah, the last survivor of his adventures in America.

"Looks like you and I are the only survivors of Tahia's fete." Teiki laughed at his family, sleeping on the couches. "

"Did you tell them about the 'Boom Boom' Vahines in Bangkok?" Tahia roared at Teiki, carrying her over his shoulder like a copra sack filled with ripe coffee beans.

"Let's go to sleep." He laughed gently laying his wife on their bed. "When you wake up, you're going to have one hell of a hangover!"

"Good morning, Hinano." Uncle Teiki whispered. "How do you feel after last night's drunken fete?"

"I have a terrible headache." She winced, taking a sip of Isaiah's coffee.

"Good morning!" Teiki grinned at his 2 grown-up children walking stiffly across the kitchen. "How do you feel this morning?"

"My head feels like a heavy coconut ready to fall off my shoulders." Tepua whispered painfully.

"I have an upset stomach." Teava said, swallowing hard.

"That's called the morning after hangover." Teiki said standing to go check on his wife. "After breakfast, we'll go to work in our fa'a'apu / taro plantation."

"In a couple of hours, your hangover will disappear."

38 ... Fa'a'apu / Taro Plantation

"How is Mama?" Tepua asked her Papa tip-toeing from their bedroom. *"She's dead to this world."* *"We'll let her sleep and check on her when we come back at lunchtime."*

The first orange and violet rays from the rising sun flickered into the Puckett Valley when Isaiah climbed into Teiki's jeep, watched Teava and Tepua mount their bareback horses, and gallop off into the early morning mist.

"You have a real quality of life in the Marquesas." Isaiah said to his Uncle driving slowly following Teava, Tepua, and Hinano leading the way on horseback.

"I hope my life with Hinano will be happy like yours with Tahia and your family in Almost Paradise."

"Hinano is an intelligent, hardworking, and loving Vahine. Mama Puckett passed her magic powers to Hinano!" Teiki said trying to help Isaiah understand his tahu'a / sorceress.

"She will use this force within her to treat the sick and defend her family. Hinano will need your help to use this power that Mama passed down from our ancestors."

38 ... Fa'a'apu / Taro Plantation

"With time, her spiritual, mental, and magic powers will become more powerful, and she will learn to control them better." Teiki chuckled stopping under a breadfruit tree.

"Just keep a close eye on her on Halloween and the nights of the full moon!"

"This is our taro plantation." He said, waving his hand across the irrigated taro paddy's filled with lush green taro leaves blowing gently in the trade winds.

"The lower half of our valley was terraced into taro paddies by the Marquesan families that lived in this valley over a 1000 years. They dug canals and sluices to divert water from our river to irrigate their taro paddies."

"Take off your tennis shoes." Teiki said handing Isaiah a wooden ironwood club resembling a softball bat with a spike on the end. *"It's easier to work barefoot in the muddy taro paddy."*

"Hi! Ho! It's off to work we go!" Teiki laughed leading his barefoot family into the muddy taro paddy. *"Let's go plant taro!"*

"Where have I seen this club before?" Isaiah asked, swinging it over his shoulder.

"You saw Luke Sandstone on television carrying this stone age club on his shoulder, dragging his Vahine by her hair to work in the taro patch." Teiki laughed at Hinano glaring at Isaiah thinking about this stone age custom. "It wasn't a patu / war club to bash his vahine on the head!"

"When we colonize the Moon, it's likely a Polynesian astronaut will use this same stone age tool we call the **tohi patia apo'o taro** / a wooden drill to punch a crater to plant taro in the Moon's soil to feed the first colony of humans."

"It was the 1st farm tool invented over 5000 years ago to plant taro in the floodplain of the Nile River."

"Taro culture was the basis of the Egyptian civilization; then carried across to Iraq, India, down the Malay Peninsula through the Philipines and Indonesia, and our Polynesian ancestors carried it across the South Pacific Ocean in their double-hulled voyaging canoes."

"Taro contains more calcium, vitamins, protein, fluoride, and minerals than mother's milk."

"The tohi weighs about the same as a softball bat with a spiked end." Teiki said hefting the stone age tool in his calloused hands.

"Lift the tohi knee-high above the ground, then drive it into the soft mud, wiggle-waggling it back and forth, forming a cone-shaped crater."

"Watch Hinano pressing the young taro shoot just enough to hold it upright in the crater."

"Tepua and Hinano will follow planting the taro shoots."

"Taro grows to maturity, ready to harvest in six to eight months."

"The green 'elephant ear' leaves we prepare as fafa / taro spinach are a complete source of vitamins A, B, C, D, and iron."

"Taro is the most nutritious food ever discovered by man."

"Last night was the first time I ever saw your Auntie Tahia get roaring drunk." Teiki said to Hinano, bouncing in the back seat while he wrestled the jeep over the muddy bush track.

"Would you check on her when we get home. She must have a terrible hangover this morning."

He pushed aside his bedroom curtain and peeked in at his beloved wife lying face down with a pillow over her head. *"If you're alive, wiggle your toes!"*

"Do you have an upset stomach?" More vigorous toe movement.

"Do you have a headache?" Teiki asked.

Auntie Tahia's ten toes wiggled frantically!

Hinano pushed past her gawking family and sat on the bed next to her Auntie.

"Would you like me to help you?"

Tahia reached back and squeezed Hinano's hand.

Hinano looked around at the crowd staring at her Auntie. *"You all go away and close the curtain."*

"We have a phone patch scheduled with your Dad." Teiki said, checking his watch and looking at Isaiah.

"While Tepua and Teava prepare lunch, we'll make our phone patch to your Dad."

223

"Bring your notebook computer with you." Teiki said, leading Isaiah to his ham radio shack, closed the steel door, and took his seat next to Isaiah, setting up his computer.

"Tell me about this mysterious marine science research project Hinano said you want me to help you with?"

*****

39 ... A New Centurion Satellite!

"CQ! CQ!" Teiki called into his microphone, inviting a reply from his ham radio contact on Nantucket Island. *"This is Fo5zz on of Nuku Hiva in the Marquesas Islands, making a phone patch to Joshua Puckett on Nantucket Island."*

"Good evening! This is Joshua Puckett on Nantucket Island standing by for your phone patch."

"Kaoha nui i te henua enana! / Greetings from the Land of Humans in the equatorial South Pacific Ocean." Teiki grinned at Isaiah, listening to his Father's deep voice resonating around the steel container.

"I'm your Cousin Teiki Puckett from Nuku Hiva in the Marquesas Islands."

"I'm happy to make your acquaintance, Cousin Teiki." Joshua laughed. *"You speak excellent English."*

"I spent 5 years in America. Marquesan is our native language at home, but we upgrade and practice our English with passing yachties who stop over and visit with us."

"I'm a descendant of Toma Puckett, who sailed to the Marquesas Islands in 1859 to work for an English trading company logging and exporting rose and sandalwood from our rainforests."

"Toma worked for the logging crews until a Marquesan warrior chief killed him after he caught him in the act with his vahine." Teiki laughed, concluding his chapter of the Marquesan Puckett family.

"They cooked him in a ground oven and served him at a feast to celebrate their victory over their enemy."

"Pirates, and now cannibals!" Joshua laughed over the phone patch. "We sure have an interesting family history."

"I'll pass the microphone to Isaiah and talk to you later." Teiki smiled at his cousin.

"Hello! Dad." Isaiah said, happy to hear his Father's voice.

"Hello! Son. Tell me your adventures with Uncle Teiki in the Marquesas."

"Uncle Teiki and his family live in a remote valley on Nuku Hiva Island accessible by risking life and limb in a wild jeep ride down a mountain."

"Uncle Teiki is the same age as you, Dad. He's a short, muscular Marquesan Warrior Chief covered head to bare feet with Tahitian, Hawaiian, Maori, and Samoan tattoos."

"He came to America in the 1970s to search for his Puckett family, got swept up, and spent 18 months in the Vietnam War."

"Like you, Dad. He was awarded a Silver Star and Purple Heart Medal."

"He returned home to Nuku Hiva and married a beautiful 17-year-old Vahine from a neighboring valley."

"Teiki and his wife Tahia have 2 children."
"Tepua, their 18-year-old daughter; and Teava, their 22-year-old son."

"They raise a herd of milk and beef cattle, horses, goats, and pigs in their lush green Puckett Valley."

"They grow their own garden vegetables, taro, corn, tomatoes, lettuce, cucumbers; and cultivate coffee, vanilla, limes, oranges, for their own use and for sale to passing yachts."

"Uncle Teiki took me fishing in their 36-foot offshore boat they built themselves from tropical hardwoods. In four hours, we caught over a dozen skip-jack tuna, five 25 lb yellowfin tuna, and two 20 lb mahi-mahi."

"I miss you! Son. I'm very lonely living alone."
"I look forward to you and Hinano coming home and making this old white house come alive again."

"I have another surprise for you. Uncle Teiki's 22-year-old son Teava and 18-year-old daughter Tepua want to visit our Puckett family in America."

"I've invited them to spend 3 months paid 'working holiday' with you during our June, July, and August tourist season."

"Tepua can look after the tourists who rent our summer rental cottages."

"She's a great cook! Wait till you taste her grilled tuna steaks in a lime and garlic butter sauce."

"Teava's an expert fisherman and boat builder like his Dad. He can go fishing with you and work in our boat shop."

"Tepua and Teava will be safe and comfortable, working, and living with their Uncle Joshua for 3 or 4 months during our busy summer tourist season."

"A great way for them to visit and discover America."

Joshua, "What do their parents think about your invitation?"

"We think it's a great idea, Cousin!" Teiki said, grabbing the microphone.

"I'd be honored to have you, your wife, and children as my guests. Our Great-Grandfather's house is your home too. Cousin Teiki."

"Tahia and I are happy to accept your invitation!" Teiki said happily.

"We'd love to visit our American Puckett family on Nantucket Island."

Joshua, "Son, you still 'GO' with your marine research project?"

"Yes, Dad. I explained it to Uncle Teiki, and we'll be leaving in a few days for the Northern Island Group in his fishing boat."

Joshua, "The 'Tahia II' at the end of the quay?"

"How does he know that?" Teiki whispered.

"I'm looking at your ocean freight container with a 3-meter satellite antenna pointed at the equator."

"That's correct!" Teiki said, taking away the microphone. "I send and receive transmissions from a ham radio satellite over the equator."

"Turn on your satellite antenna and decoder," Joshua instructed him. "Tune to channel 12 and wait until you see a new frequency and channel on your monitor. You got it, Cousin?"

"Roger!" Teiki said, turning to the new frequency and channel.

"Increase your signal strength until you see a flashing icon indicating the two frequencies are locked and synchronized together."

"We're receiving your TV images crystal clear, and sound is booming in 5 by 5." Teiki called out, amazed at this new satellite communications technology.

"A week after you left for Tahiti, Ensign Puckett." Adml Porche said, smiling at Isaiah.

"We launched state of the art 'Centurion' satellite a few kilometers over your heads so we could follow your adventures in the Marquesas Islands."

"Two weeks ago, Sgt. Major Lopez and I flew to Nantucket Island to visit your Father."

"He gave us a well-deserved lecture on how Hoffman terrorized you and the other Ensigns under his command and tried to destroy your career in the Navy."

"A few days after you left Cmdr. Hoffman was arrested by the Shore Patrol, charged with drunk driving, and assaulting a chief petty officer in the performance of his duties."

"Hoffman was forced to resign from the Navy to avoid a court-martial."

"I destroyed Hoffman's General Discharge Papers he showed you before you left for Tahiti." Adm Porche said, sitting straight in his chair and righting an inexcusable failure in his command leadership.

"Ensign Isaiah Pucket II! On behalf of the United States Navy, I present our profound apologies for the way Hoffman mistreated you during your tour of duty at my NIC / Naval Intelligence Center."

"I've written a new OPR / Officers Performance Report on your courage, initiative, and menace the Chinese Submarine Incident poses to our National Security during your assignment in my Naval Intelligence Center endorsed by Admiral Hansen, CINCPAC / Commander."

"We consider you an outstanding young officer with a great future in the Navy if you decide to continue your career with us."

"We Pucketts have served the Nation in every conflict since our Declaration of Independence from England in 1776." Isaiah said, looking at Adm Porche.

"We've never had a general or admiral in our family. Like the Minutemen at Lexington and Concord, we Puckett's are citizen soldiers."

"When I finish my 4-year tour of duty in the Navy."

"I plan to return home like my Great Grandfather Capt Isaiah Puckett, my Father Joshua, and my Uncle Teiki."

"Your Dad told us how you flew to Tahiti to search for your Tahitian family." Adm Porche said, accepting Isaiah's decision. "What did you discover?"

"I found my 83-year-old Cousin Ahu'ura Puckett living in a dilapidated plantation home built by my Great-Grandfather for his beloved wife Hinareva in 1840. Mama showed me her family genealogy tracing her roots back 150 years to our common ancestors."

"She and her adopted granddaughter Hinano gave me Capt Puckett's Navy sextant and pirate's cutlass he used during the War of 1812."

"Mama returned my Great Grandfather's 'Secret Journal,' describing the wreck of a Spanish galleon laden with Inca gold lost on a coral reef in the Tuamotu Islands during a fierce tropical cyclone in the 1600s."

"Did Capt Puckett recover the Spanish treasure?" Adm Porche asked.

"He found the lost galleon and his Tuamotu pearl divers brought up a few gold coins and ingots."

"The wreck was too deep for his divers to continue without risking death from the bends / nitrogen paralysis."

"Capt Puckett recorded his search in a 'Secret' Navy Code he used during the War of 1812."

"He left the lost Spanish treasure as a challenge for his male descendants."

"When I finish my active duty in the Navy."
"I want to sail with my Dad and Uncle Teiki to the Tuamotu Atolls and search for my Great Grandfather's treasure."

"When I return to Hawaii, I'd like your help to find the lost code in the Navy's War of 1812 archives and decipher Capt Puckett's Secret Journal."

"I've never seen or deciphered a 1812 Navy code." The Chief of Naval Intelligence said, laughing at the thought.

"Helping you guys recover the treasure of the Spanish galleon sounds like a real challenge and adventure."

"The Navy has lots of experience recovering lost submarines, ships, and nuclear weapons in the oceanic depths."

"When you finish your intelligence gathering mission and return to Hawaii, we'll discuss your treasure hunt with Adm Hansen."

"His wife, Tahia's family, owns ancestral land in the Northern Island Group 15 kilometers from the underground Chinese missile base."

"Every 4 to 6 months, he takes his family on their fishing boat to Tahia's island for a 2-week working holiday in her valley to work their plantation."

"Care for their horses and cattle, go fishing, cut tropical woods for their fishing boat, and upgrade their bungalows."

"Uncle Teiki thinks the Chinese have his fishing boat and family logged on their surveillance records as non-hostile natives that stop a couple of hours to fish for red snapper and grouper in the 'Blue Hole.'"

"So long as we don't linger too long or go ashore, we pose no danger to them. They have to stay hidden to keep their secret."

"My Uncle Teiki knows the sea and terrain around the objective. He's best qualified to plan and lead my recon mission."

"I have your Uncle's 'Army Personnel Records," Marine Sgt Major Pete Lopez said, grinning at the deeply tanned barefoot Marquesan sitting next to Ensign Puckett.

"I need a positive ID for his security clearance."

"Does he have a sea turtle tattoo on his shoulder?"

"Affirmative." Isaiah said, grinning at his Uncle tugging on his goatee. *"And some buckshot scars on his butt from an irate husband who caught him in bed with his young wife."*

"You confirm his identity." Sgt. Major Lopez said, grinning at the wily Marquesan Billy Goat.

"S/Sgt. Teiki Puckett, US Army, Honorable Discharge, awarded the Purple Heart and Silver Star."

"What's the name of Tahia's Island?" Admiral Porche asked, clicking down a satellite image of the northern group of tiny volcanic islands and lava rock pinnacles rising above the South Pacific Ocean.

"Motu Henua Mana / Sacred Island of our Ancestors." Teiki said, studying the close-up satellite images.

"Tahia's island is riddled with lava tubes and underground caves our Marquesan ancestors used to bury their Haka'iki/ High Chiefs like the Egyptians entombed their Pharaohs in Valley of Kings."

"The Northern Marquesas Islands were inhabited until the Spanish, English, French, and American whalers brought in the plague, smallpox, and flu epidemics killed off the pure race Marquesans with no natural resistance to the imported European diseases."

"The surviving Marquesan families withdrew to the major Islands of Nuku Hiva, Hiva Oa, and Tahiti."

"Today there are no permanent residents in the Northern Group of Islands." Teiki said recounting the tragic history of the Islands.

"But they are still visited by families that own ancestral lands on them."

"Six years ago, a family of five Marquesans, their fishing boat, and bungalow disappeared without a trace." Teiki recounted angrily.

"Ensign Puckett solved the mystery when he showed me the Chinese submarine going into the 'Blue Hole' lava tube under the ancient volcano.

"The Chinese invaders killed a Marquesan family simply because they got too close to their secret." Teiki roared into the microphone.

"The Chinese invaded my country and drew first blood!"

"We will seek them out and make them taste the fire and fury of 'Oro,' our ancient god of war!"

"I swear this oath on the sacred marae/temple of our ancestors!"

"Hoo! Haaa! Hee!, Hoo! Haaa! Hee!" Teiki roared again, pounding the table with his fists.

"What the hell was that?" Adm Porche demanded.

"The ancient war chant of our Marquesan warriors before they went into battle!" Teiki roared again, glaring at Adm Porche.

"When my ancestors went into battle against an invader, they killed their enemies in hand to hand combat with a flat oval-shaped patu / war club."

"The Warrior Chief tanned their enemies heads and sent them back to their island as a warning of the fate awaiting those who followed."

"Did they eat their slain enemies?" Sgt. Major Lopez asked remembering the Marquesian's historical reputation for their fearless tattooed warriors who feasted on their enemies to celebrate their victories.

"Slain enemy warriors were gutted like pigs, seasoned with native spices, wrapped in banana leaves, smoked in a ground oven until the meat was tender and juicy!"

"Long Pig was carved in morsels and served in umetes to the chief and his warriors at their victory feast." Teiki said making a loud slurping sound, and giving everyone his best cannibal grin!

"My Grandfather said 'Long Pig' had lean meat and the same taste as our short Marquesan pig."

*"After reading newspaper reports about our last Marquesan war, **Theodore Roosevelt** copied our strategy in his famous speech."*

"Speak softly and carry a big patu / stick."

"Tomorrow morning, we'll load the 'Tahia II' with provisions for a two week holiday on Motu Henua Mana." Teiki said, laying out his Coast-watcher Plan for Adm Porche and Sgt. Major Lopez.

"Tomorrow afternoon, we'll begin the 6-hour sea voyage to Motu Henua Mana."

"A Chinese Missile Base on Motu Henua Mana poses a direct nuclear menace to the United States." Adm Porche said looking seriously at Teiki.

"We have a 'National Security Priority' for men, money, and assets to accomplish this Coastwatcher Mission."

Teiki paused a long moment to reflect on Adm Porche's offer, and looked at Isaiah. "Admirals right, this Coastwatcher Mission is too much for you and me."

"Search through your Department of Defense personnel records for South Pacific Islanders serving as Navy Seals, Army Green Berets, and Marine Jungle Warriors for this mission."
Teiki said to Adm Porche and Sgt. Major Lopez listening to his proposal.

"I want tough Polynesian Warriors who can slip barefoot through the jungle and kill their enemies in silent hand to hand combat like their ancestors."

"American Samoans, Hawaiians, Tahitians, who grew up in the islands, and speak their languages."

"Buy eight 6 man offshore outrigger canoes made from the epoxy laminated wood strip and carbon fiber, like the Vaa used in the annual Molokai to Waikiki Beach ocean race held each year in October."

"I want tough Polynesian Warriors who can launch their war canoes at night, paddle 15 kilometers on top of oceanic swells breaking on the high volcanic cliffs."
Teiki said, laying out his tactical operations plan.

"Land their canoes silently under cover of night, and accomplish our intelligence gathering tasks on the volcanic cone without being detected by the enemy."

"I'll spend two nights training them at our Base Camp before we attack our objective."

"We'll conduct our ancient war chants and dances to make us spiritually and mentally stronger, and invisible to our enemies."

"Our mission is to collect intelligence data on the secret Chinese underground missile base and present it to the President's White House National Security Adviser." Adm Porche said firmly.

"Not engage them in combat and start WWIII."

"I want my Cousin, former US Navy Lt. Joshua Puckett, called to active duty as our' Operations Officer." Teiki said looking at Adm Porche and Sgt. Major Lopez. "He led intelligence gathering missions in Vietnam. Joshua has the combat and leadership experience we need to plan and lead this Coastwatcher Mission."

"The lives of millions of Americans are at stake," Joshua said, giving Adm Porche a hard look. "We have to prevail on this Coastwatcher Mission or perish."

"What do you think?" Adm Porche asked Sgt Major Lopez.

"These are your words, Admiral." The Marine said. "This mission is too complex and dangerous for two persons."

"Can you find someone to look after your home and business for a couple of weeks?" Adm Porche asked.

Joshua, "I'll telephone my friend Paul Garrett and ask him to look after my home and boat while I'm off on holiday to visit my Son in Hawaii."

"My fellow Veterans will look after my fishing boat while I am gone."

"Welcome back in the US Navy, Cmdr Puckett." Adm Porche said smiling at his new Operations Officer.

"I'll have a Navy jet on the tarmac at Nantucket Airport in three hours to fly you to Hawaii."

Sgt Major Lopez. "I'll meet you at Pearl Harbor' Naval Air Station."

"We'll run you through a quick medical exam at the Navy Hospital and give you a few hours to catch up on your sleep credits for this mission."

"We'll need a few days to assemble your Polynesians, and load them in the Nuclear Attack Submarine' Manta Ray' being readied for this Coastwatcher Mission."

"When you take your fishing boat over to Motu Henua Mana, we'll track you with our Centurion satellite." Adm Porche said, smiling at his Marquesan Warrior Chief.

Teiki. "I'll paint our ancient pathfinder god Honu / Sea Turtle on the foredeck so you can follow us with your satellite."

"How big should I paint it?"

"About the size of the turtle tattoo on your shoulder."

"Wow!" Teiki exclaimed. "That good?"

"Better!" Adm Porche laughed.

"I'm not sure how we'll fit your 8-meter war canoes into the submarine?" Sgt Major Lopez mused looking at Teiki. "They may be too long to go through the cargo hatches."

"Cut them in half with a chainsaw!" Teiki said grinning at the Marine. "We'll join the halves together at our Base Camp with bamboo strips, carbon fiber cloth, and quick-drying epoxy."

"Teiki has a Marquesan solution to every problem." Adm Porche laughed. "Is there anything special you want for your family from Hawaii?"

Teiki, "My Son and I built two new bungalows on Motu Henua Mana. We need two new toilets to complete our throne room."

Adm Porche. "Anything else you would like for your family?"

"Our Vahines love Hawaiian shampoo, monoi, and bright, colorful Hawaiian fabrics to make tablecloths curtains, and patchwork bedspreads."

"His family loves gourmet ice cream!" Isaiah interjected. "It's a rare treat they get once a year when they fly to Tahiti."

"What flavors do they like?" Sgt. Major Lopez asked, laughing at Isaiah's delicious idea.

"Coconut! Boysenberry! Strawberry! Guava! Mango! and Macadamia Nut!" Teiki said happily.

"We'll fill Manta Ray's freezer with Hawaii's finest gourmet ice cream." Sgt. Major Lopez said, watching Teiki break into a mouthwatering smile.

"Don't forget to bring several cases of Uncle Teiki's 'Old Pirate Rum 'and 'Chinese BBQ Sauce' for the victory feast when we complete your recon mission." Isaiah said to Adm Porche and Sgt. Major Lopez indicating it was time to close down the sat com link.

"I look forward to our visit, Son." Joshua said farewell from Nantucket Island. *"Give my future daughter in law a goodnight kiss for me."*

"We look forward to meeting you and your family in person. This is Adm Porche and Sgt. Major Lopez saying 'Farewell' from Hawaii."

Teiki and Isaiah watched the computer screen turn to electronic snow, and once again, the speaker filling the ham radio shack with space noise and static.

"Give me a minute to shut down my ham radio, satellite receiver, and we'll join Tahia at the waterfall."

*****

40 ... An Ancient Toa / Warrior Chief

"How high is your waterfall?" Isaiah asked, following Uncle Teiki to his faithful jeep parked next to the horse trough.

"It cascades 300 feet off the plateau." Teiki said, starting the engine and driving across the coconut plantation. *"After a heavy thunderstorm in the mountains, it's quite spectacular cascading down the sheer walls into a natural pool at the bottom of the gorge."*

"I'm sure our Vahines and Teava are having a great time swimming in the double rainbow under the waterfall."

"Tell me more about the lost Spanish galleon, gold coins, and coral-encrusted ingots Capt Puckett found in the Tuamotu Atolls." Teiki said, driving into the narrow bush track alongside the river rushing down his valley. *"Going on a treasure hunt sounds like it would be another great Puckett Adventure!"*

"Let's stop a few minutes at our family marae." Teiki said, driving into the ancient ruins, and parking next to two moss-covered stone Tiki standing lonely vigil over the marae.

"Our family has a place reserved on this marae when the haka-iki / high chiefs called the clans together for an important ceremony."
The Marquesan Warrior Chief said, leading Isaiah onto the stone plaza.

"This vertical basalt turu'i / totem is reserved for the warrior chief of my family." Teiki said, pointing to a petroglyph of a honu / sacred sea turtle engraved on the 8-foot basalt turu'i/ totem.

"When you told me your secret mission was to   seek out the Chinese missile base on Motu Henua Mana." Teiki sat in front of the Turi, rocking on his heels, staring into his nephew's eyes.

"I had a vision of your Father, You, and I stood before a war council of Haka Iki / High Chiefs on this great stone plaza with 100's of warrior spirits who fell in combat driving enemy invaders from our islands."

"Our Marquesan Toa / Warrior Chief Pokoko wearing his te avaha / warriors headdress decorated with a pearl and turtle shell emblem, red and white feathers, raised his patu to demand silence, and began his oration."

"Te Henua Enana has been invaded by foreigners from the East!" The ancient Toa /Warrior Spirit proclaimed. "They killed a family from Nuku Hiva and desecrated our ancestral tombs on Motu Henua Mana / our Sacred Island!"

"The ancient Toa began a war dance and chant calling down the wrath of our gods on our enemies." Teiki said recounting his vivid vision.

"When the battle-scarred Toa / Warrior Chief completed his chants and orations, he marched up to your Father, You, and I standing in front of our Turu'i / family totem."

"To defeat the invaders from the east, you must be spiritually, physically, and mentally stronger!"

"You have the blood and fighting spirit of your ancestors!

"Drive our enemies from our Islands!"
The ancient Toa / Warrior Chief ordered us.
"Restore peace and harmony to Te Henua Enana / the Land of Humans!"

"What happened next?" Isaiah demanded his Uncle nodding his head from side to side while the vision slowly faded away.

"I woke up!" Teiki said, blinking his eyes.

"Are you ready to join our family in the waterfall?" He laughed, pulling his young American Warrior to his feet and leading him back through the ancient temple.

"Let's roll." Teiki said, giving a farewell salute to the two stone-faced Tiki standing eternal guard over the ancient temple and driving up the verdant valley to the waterfall.

Where his family was swimming under a brilliant double rainbow, shining through the clouds of mist swirling through the giant bamboo encircling the crystal clear waters.

*****

41 ... Nantucket Island

"Nantucket Police Department." The Front Desk Officer asked. *"Can I help you?"*

"This is Joshua Puckett. I want to speak to Chief Garrett."

"Good evening, Joshua. How are you?"

"I'm fine, Paul. I'm leaving tonight for Hawaii. I'd like you to look after my home and fishing boat for a couple of weeks."

"I'll have a patrol visit your home every day to feed your Shetland ponies and ask the guys at our Veterans Club to look after your fishing boat."

"Would you like a ride to the airport?" Chief Garrett offered his fellow Vietnam Veteran.

"I'd really appreciate that, Paul. I'll lock up this old white house and wait for you down by the front gate."

By the light of a full moon, Joshua carried his flight bags across the beach grass lawn to the white picket fence separating his front yard from the sandy track that ran downhill to Nantucket Town.

249

Thirty minutes later, Joshua watched Chief Garrett's police car drive up the sandy bluff and stop at the front gate.

"Here are the keys to my house, boat shop, and fishing boat." Joshua said, tossing his flight bags in the back seat.

"Three hours ago, I began receiving phone calls from the airport manager and air controller." Paul said, driving out to nearby Nantucket Airport. *"About a top priority Navy jet landing any moment."*

"All commercial and private and commercial flights were delayed or rerouted to Martha's Vineyard."

"The order came from the FAA and Pentagon."

"Scared the hell out of the airport manager and air controllers who flooded my front desk with phone calls wanting to know if this was an orange terrorist alert!"

"Then, my good friend Joshua calls me to look after his home while he goes on vacation to Hawaii." Paul said, driving behind the Nantucket Airport Terminal, and stopping next to a twin-engine Navy jet with its navigation lights flashing in the frosty New England night.

A young Navy pilot dashed over to the police car and looked anxiously at the uniformed Police Chief. "I'm here to pick up Cmdr Joshua Puckett and fly him to the Pearl Harbor Naval Air Station."

"I guess that's me!" Joshua replied, surprised at being addressed by his new rank.

"Do you have any ID or flight orders? Sir." The young Navy Officer asked politely.

"I am the Chief of Police of Nantucket Island!" Chief Garrett growled at the young Navy Pilot. "I assure you this is Navy Cmdr Joshua Puckett!"

The startled young Navy Pilot stepped back saluting Chief Garrett and Joshua. "Let me help you with your flight bags, Cmdr Puckett."

"This envelope contains our 'Last Will and Testament." Joshua said, handing Paul a large brown envelope. "If the Navy reports Isaiah or me missing in action or dead, give it to our lawyer Paul Thompson?"

"I'll keep in touch with you by Email mail from CINCPAC Hawaii. My Cousin Nellie will look after the 'Old Pirate's Ghost' while I'm gone."

"I'm sure I'll have a 'Whale of a Tale' to tell you guys at our monthly veterans' beer and pizza party!" Joshua promised.

"We're planning a family reunion and clambake on the beach with my Tahitian and Marquesan family when we return from this mission.

"You and your family are invited to the fete!" Cmdr Puckett called out waving 'Farewell,' before boarding the Navy jet.

"God be with you, Joshua and Isaiah Puckett." Paul Garret whispered, watching the Navy jet streak down the runway, lift off into the starlit sky, bank slowly west, and race the Hawaiian moon across the Great South Pacific Ocean.

The End

Volume One

The Chinese Submarine Incident

Volume Two

The Pucket Adventure

Discover Ensign Puckett's secret mission to uncover a Chinese IRBM missile base hidden inside an ancient volcanic cone, in a uninhabited island in the Marquesas Islands that is a direct nucllear threat to Hawaii, San Diego, Los Angeles, Seattle and San Francisco.

42 .. My Biography

Suzanne, Dick, Bernadette

I was born in 1939 Stoughton MA, 20 miles south of Boston one month after Hitler invaded Poland.

During WWII my father Richard worked as a welder in the Fall River Shipyard while my Mother Irene worked in the Shawmut Mill making military uniforms.

My four Polish Uncles fought as infantrymen in Europe and my two Italian Uncles fought in the Navy in the Pacific. Their example inspired me to carry on this proud family tradition when it was my turn.

I have cherished memories growing up at our summer cottage on Wellfleet, Cape Cod, Mass. Beachcombing with my Dad and brother Paul, after a fierce Atlantic Hurricane littered our beaches with driftwood, broken lobster traps, fishnets, and lost dories

Whale watching atop the dunes when the great whales make their annual migration from their feeding grounds off Newfoundland to the Tropic of Cancer

A half-century later, Herman Melville's *Moby Dick* and James A Michener's *Tales Of The South Pacific*, and Tom Clancey's *Military Thrillers*, would inspire me to write my *Puckett Adventure*.

A collection of five historical novels inspired by our Great American Whaling Era 1700 to 1880.

In 1955 when the post-WWII economic boom went bust in New England, my Dad loaded his family into our car and a U-Haul trailer. We drove cross country to the oil and cattle City of Wichita Falls, TX, where a new job awaited him.

In 1963 I graduated from Midwestern University with a BSc in math, physics, engineering, botany, and an ROTC commission in the US ARMY.

255

In 1964 I spent the next 13 months as a platoon leader in America's unfinished war, 8th US Army Korea.

In 1965 I was assigned to the historic Springfield Armory, Massachusetts as an R&D Project Engineer working on helicopter weapons for the Vietnam War.

In 1966 I flew the M60 Machinegun Door Gun against the enemy in Vietnam.

I volunteered for the Vietnam War and spent the next 19 months as a Captain MACV Adviser in the Mekong Delta.

After 4 ½ years in the US Army, 2 ½ years in Korea and the Vietnam War.

I decided to invest my saved up combat pay and spend a year, backpacking across the 'peaceful' South Pacific Ocean, Acapulco, Tahiti, Fiji, New Hebrides, New Caledonia, and motorcycle across Australia's Nullarbor Desert to Perth, chasing Sheilas and kangaroos!

I spent a month with **Bob Paul, a WW II Australian Coastwatcher**, on the Island of Tanna, New Hebrides now Vanuatu.

Visited **John Frum Cargo Cult** and climbed active **Yasur Volcano.**

During my 1969 backpack adventure, I met a magnificent 17-year-old Vahine Tahiti on the Island of Moorea.

Her name is **Bernadette**. We've been married 54 years and made Raiatea our island home for more than 30 years.

I spend most of my retirement time, with my family in Uturoa Village, working on my South Pacific adventure and romance novels, TV Movies, and major theatrical movies set in Tahiti and Hawaii.

Richard (Dick) Sarcione

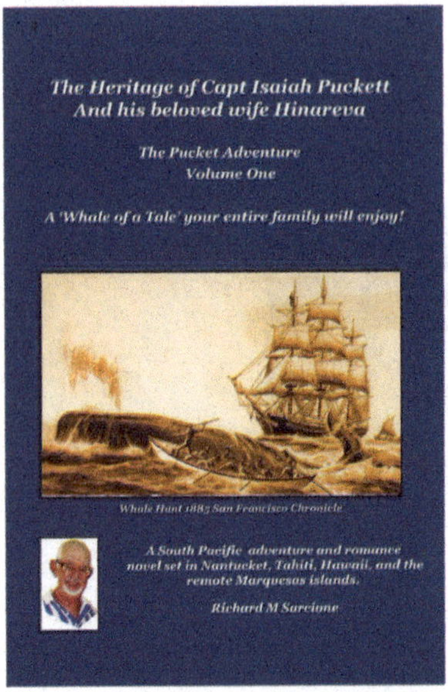

258

The Heritage of Capt Isaiah Puckett And his beloved wife Hinareva

The Puckett Adventure
Volume One

A 'Whale of a Tale' your entire family will enjoy!

Whale Hunt 1885 San Francisco Chronicle

A South Pacific adventure and romance novel set in Nantucket, Tahiti, Hawaii, and the remote Marquesas islands.

Richard M Sarcione

The Chinese Submarine Incident

The Puckett Adventure
Volume Two

A South Pacific 'Thriller' your entire family will enjoy!

Discover Ensign Puckett's secret mission to uncover a Chinese IRBM missile base inside an ancient volcanic cone that is a direct nuclear threat to Hawaii, Seattle, San Francisco, Los Angeles, and San Diego.

Richard M Sarcione

The Coastwatcher Mission

Volume Three
Puckett Adventure

"Fall in and line up on me." She said back paddling, and waiting for the right wave to rise under her lead canoe.

"Go! Go! Go!" Lt. Puckett said urgently to her war party poised to surf their outrigger canoes down a giant oceanic swell rising up and hurling towards the narrow strip of black sand beach.

Isaiah grunted paddling furiously down the breaking wave surfing their war canoes high on the beach. "This is what our Capt Puckett called a Nantucket sleigh ride!"

Battle Stations

Volume Four
Puckett Adventure

Isaiah, 'Hundreds of Chinese Marines, with AK 47's are climbing into their landing craft and lowered over the side into the water.'

"I can hear a loud, Whoop! Whoop! Whoop! reverberating across the water."

"Adm Chang is sounding 'Battle Stations!'" Joshua said turning up the volume on the sat com net.

259

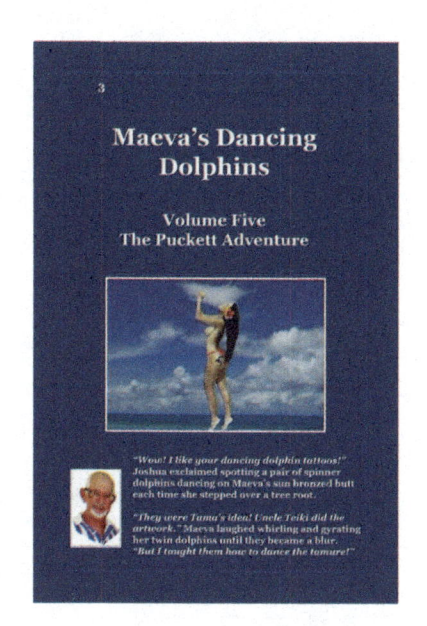

Maeva's Dancing Dolphins

Volume Five
The Puckett Adventure

"Wow! I like your dancing dolphin tattoos!" Joshua exclaimed spotting a pair of spinner dolphins dancing on Maeva's sun bronzed butt each time she stepped over a tree root.

"They were Tama's idea! Uncle Teiki did the artwork." Maeva laughed whirling and gyrating her twin dolphins until they became a blur. "But I taught them how to dance the tamure!"

Made in the USA
Columbia, SC
27 October 2023